**DIVIDED BY WAR, UNITED BY PASSION, THEY DARED TO LOVE. . . .**

**ZARA**—Exotically beautiful and untamed, she would defy her heritage to possess the man she loved.

**RAIF**—Sensitive, tender, his belief in peace could not save him from a violent passion.

**MICHA**—Handsome and hot-tempered, he came to desire Zara enough to destroy her rather than lose her.

**RUTH**—A proud survivor of the Nazi horror, she would stop at nothing to keep her daughter from marrying the enemy.

**RONAR**—Tanned, lithe, mysterious, he watched the land with a soldier's strength . . . and Zara with a man's unquenchable desire.

**"HEARTBREAK, HORROR, AND FIERCE LOVE."**
—*Kirkus Reviews*

**"A PORTRAIT OF A REMARKABLE HEROINE."**
—*The Chattanooga Times*

# CHANGING
# STATES

## Barbara Rogan

A DELL BOOK

Published by
Dell Publishing Co., Inc.
1 Dag Hammarskjold Plaza
New York, New York 10017

Dell ® TM 681510, Dell Publishing Co., Inc.

ISBN: 0-440-11049-1

Reprinted by arrangement with Doubleday & Company, Inc.

Printed in the United States of America

First Dell printing—February 1983

For Tillie Fisher and Pauline Riemer, and in memory of
Max Rogan and Morris Riemer

# PART I
---
# ISRAEL

# CHAPTER I

Two boys wanted her but her true lover, whose steady gaze gave growth and warmth, was the sun. At fifteen she was taller than her mother and father, slim, golden-haired, brown, green-eyed, and beautiful of face. She was no longer Hope. She was Zara, and the boy who had renamed her in scorn now pursued her in lust or love.

The name happened a few weeks after Hope and her family moved into their new home in the Galilee village of Tivon. On a hot morning in early September, Mediterranean sun scorching the scattered white stone houses, the olive trees, scrub bushes, and dirt roads that were now her home, Hope's first day of school was her last day as Hope. She walked to school alone, skirting the village, taking the long way round through the hills. The Israeli school uniform of light blue cotton shirt and navy blue shorts felt light on her. On her back, Israeli-style, was an empty book satchel, and she clutched a slip of paper with her fourth-grade classroom number and teacher's name. The stark

openness of this new place was awesome: no buildings to
cradle her, just the cloudless open sky with its burning eye
to cover her, and this awful purging heat, rising from the
ground and descending from the sky, to hold her. What
would save her if one of those circling hawks spotted her
crossing the hill all alone, swooped down and carried her
off? Even the school, when she reached it, was exposed,
windows flung wide and sky-blue, children leaning from
windows toward friends like plants to the sun, calling out to
each other in raucous bursts of Hebrew. Hope found her
classroom and took a seat in the back. The other children,
chattering in groups, ignored her, so she looked at them.
They were nearly all dark-haired, dusky-skinned sabras.
She felt conspicuous. One tall boy, brown-haired with a
handsome foxy face, stared at her unsmilingly, then said
something to his friends that made them smirk. The girl in
the front of the room, whom Hope had guessed was a high
school monitor, called them to order. "I'm a soldier and
your teacher this year. My name is Noemi. As I call out
your names, answer 'Here.' " Hope had learned enough
Hebrew in their summertime language course to understand, but she was shy of speaking with her American
accent. In the *ulpan* in Tel Aviv, they'd told her that her
name had a beautiful Hebrew translation and that she would
be called by it: Tikva. Her anger at their tampering with her
name was lessened by the fact that she had grown tired of
Hope, and Tikva being foreign, less would be expected of
her.

"Tikva," the teacher called for the second time and,
startled from a memory, Hope responded in English. The
class roared, and the fox-faced boy, who'd sat next to her,
said to a friend, "Our first English lesson," in a la-di-da
accent. Noemi pounded her desk for quiet.

"Tikva's family has recently moved here from the U.S., and they now live in Tivon. Tikva studied Hebrew in an ulpan this summer and she did very well, but of course she doesn't know Hebrew perfectly yet. I'm sure you'll all be helpful."

"Of course we will, Teacher," intoned the boy, and though he made them all laugh at her again, Hope sensed that his intent was not completely malignant. At recess she was surrounded and interrogated in spitfire Hebrew. The first question came from Tsipi, the stunning almond-eyed, olive-skinned girl whose looks Hope had chosen to envy the moment she laid eyes on her. "How come your name's Tikva if you're from America?"

"My name was Hope, so they changed it to Tikva."

"Some Tikva," mocked the fox-faced boy. He mocked beautifully. His name was Micha, and he commanded troops in the fourth grade. "Tikva zara," he said. The children roared with laughter, and for the rest of the day, except in the teacher's hearing, they called her Tikva Zara. Hope wasn't sure what the second word meant, and after recess looked it up in her desk dictionary. It was the feminine form of "Zar": foreign or strange. Foreign Hope, they'd named her, Strange Hope; and the name, though intended to mock, gave her the thrill of pleasure that a lost dog feels on hearing his name called.

These were the things Zara knew about herself. She was special. She was her mother's Hope. She was the daughter of survivors, which made her a survivor too; and she'd always known that. She was the Lone Ranger, at least in her dream life. She owned a recurrent dream. Always in the beginning she was the Lone Ranger, the masked man making his lonely way through the vast West, punctuating his journey with acts of grace and goodness, rewarded only by the grateful, loving farewells of the saved. But where is the Lone Ranger going? What he does is clear enough, but what is his destination?

He doesn't seem to have one. The Lone Ranger is just wandering, with no stopping place, no possible end, no rest. (As a sense of sorrow pervades the dream, Hope's point of view lifts; she is no longer the Lone Ranger but a disembodied presence close to him.)

Now his enemies close in on him, drawing ever nearer in a horse chase through canyons and gullies. Suddenly (proving the inferiority of dreams to television) the Lone Ranger is caught! Caught, overpowered, and pinned helpless to the earth. The head villain approaches, twirling his moustache and crossing his eyes. "Hold him, boys," he growls, and laughing evilly, he reaches down and rips the mask from the Lone Ranger's face. Then all freeze in horror, for what is revealed is nothing like what was expected. They see not a scarred face, nor one purified by suffering and atonement; no, they see a face rotting with age, the ravaged, bombed-out face of an old, old man.

Like a secret name, a dream all her own (though the giver was mysterious) signaled ascension to a higher plane, an advance of selfhood. Sensing this, Hope loved her dream, cherished it even for its moment of terrible revelation. Though her dream had a scorpion's tail, still it was her own, a self-formulation.

She knew too that the name her mother called her was true only for Ruth, and that her natural name was the one Micha had divined. He was not the first. Carmen had been.

When she lived in New York, Zara used to play a game of her own invention, called Invisibility. Rarely attacked (except by their specific predators and peers), rarely even noticed, city children are a special class, and of course they know it. But exemption from violence is not given, but earned through proper street behavior, and this Hope practiced in the game of her invention, played alone. She won whenever she remained completely unnoticed while in plain sight. Best played at dusk, since children out alone after dark were highly visible, the game required no special equipment, just sneakers, ordinary clothes, and a mental cloak. Hope was good at it. On days when she visited the park without playing the game, people always spoke to her: vendors who called out, "Hello, sweetheart," old ladies, or other kids. But the only people who ever noticed her when she played the game were those whose own invisibility quotient was high: ghosts spotting other ghosts.

One day, stalking a young couple through the park, playing not just Invisibility but a variant of it, Invisible Tiger, Hope sensed the man about to turn around. She quickly sat down on a nearby bench and fiddled with her shoelaces. To her astonishment, a woman sitting right next to her, whom she hadn't even noticed, said hello to her.

It meant she'd lost. But Hope answered politely, "Hello."

"Did I spoil your game?"

"Kind of, but that's all right." She added respectfully, "Most people don't know I'm playing one."

The woman smiled. "Takes one to know one." She was a dark woman, black hair and eyes and the trace of a foreign-overlaid-by-New York accent. She closed her book and held out a bag. "Have a caramel?"

"Thanks." Hope was fascinated. "I'm Hope," she said hopefully.

"That's funny, I thought you were despair."

Hope laughed delightedly; no one had ever made such a grown-up joke to her before. "No, I meant my name."

"Where'd you get such sad eyes from, then?"

She answered a serious question seriously. "From my parents."

"And where'd they get theirs?"

Then Hope did a sly thing: exposed a secret to a stranger, hoping for enlightenment. "From Hitler," she dared, and was daunted by the lady's gasp and her averted eyes. She jumped up. "I gotta go now, lady. . . ."

"No, wait," said the lady, catching her with her eyes. "If you go now, I'll be hopeless. And you—since my name is Faith—would be faithless."

Halfway across the park, Hope got it. Stopped in her tracks, giggled, and went back to the bench where the woman still sat.

"That was a good one," she said. "Is your name really Faith, or did you just say that for the joke?"

"I said it for the joke. My name's really Carmen. And is yours really Hope or were your parents kidding?"

This she did not, would not, understand; but some involuntary comprehension made her queasy. She said stoically, "Hope's my real name."

The woman said nothing more, but Hope, who had not yet learned that she couldn't, distinctly heard her think, "Strange Hope."

Now, knowing that Micha had called her rightly, she accepted the new name.

By the next day, it was just Zara that they called her and she answered to, and so it went until the Tikva just dried up and dropped off, until, outside of her home, where she was still and forever Hope, she was no one but Zara.

The name had grafted well, grown into a person, Zara, who was not Hope. Flung eastward by wandering Jew parents, dropped into the dusty brown-and-gray bowl of hot winds, pure light, seasonal drought and flood, she'd found it an easing landscape. The rigor of climatic conditions satiated her need for expressed conflict so she could be quieter within. The little-rained-upon land, whose survival came from underground springs, soothed her with its unexamined familiarity; the yearly drought, the constant siege fed her spirit which had wilted with overwatering. And the dangers of New York: lurching crazies, spawned of slackness and overabundance, thoroughbred consumers teased too far, madmen who appeared out of the crowd without warning so that survival dictated a back-to-the-wall stance; these she traded gladly for the natural dangers of her new home: scorpions, vipers, fire, and flood. Here she stood free and let the dry wind sculpt her body in the round, blowing away sedentary fat, carving her lean and lithe but also forming surprising roundnesses of breast and hip, just as the frugal Mideastern earth splurged vital water on lush oases.

This fifteen-year-old Zara broke forth from school every day at one o'clock and rushed outside like a diver rising for air, shed her schoolbag at home, snatched a sandwich, and ran to the hills or the wadi or beyond. She usually made her trips alone, though sometimes Micha, her only school friend, came too. Not well-liked, this Zara, she didn't care at all, but thought herself more talented in enmity than in friendship. At fifteen she had an acceptable prettiness that stood on the brink of unmanageable beauty; she had an unwillingness to yield, considered unbecoming to a girl who should be preparing for marriage, a body that treacherously combined enticing softness and unwonted muscular strength, an inability to squeal girlishly but a readiness to fight seriously. Being all that, she had no need to do anything disgraceful to garner peer contempt. But to top it off, there was her persistent, and unheard of, refusal to join a youth group.

That, too, began during her first weeks in Tivon. It was another seething day—the sun so bright she was blind without sunglasses. She'd brought to school a pack with canteen, sandwich, and fruit, and worn a bathing suit under her clothes. She'd watched the clock throughout the last agonizing lesson in Bible and then, at one, they were set free. Zara ran down the hill on which Tivon was built, to explore the wadi below.

Started running—but outside the burning sun enforced temperance: calmness, lowered eyes, and an unhurried stride were required. Inside the wadi's oak- and pine-shaded depth the sunlight was diffused and liquefied. A moist green smell rose up around her as she parted reeds and stepped on water-polished stones, seeking the water which was nearly all gone by the end of summer. She followed the signs of the water's passage deeper into the wadi, up a gentle slope toward the source. The earthen walls were steep and close around her, and the smell and sound of water grew strong. She passed a few unevaporated pools of no more than a foot in depth. Had she not heard voices, she would never have found the hidden pool, which was set into one of the wadi's walls, concealed by tall reeds. But hearing voices, she followed them, crawling on hands and knees through a gap in the reeds. Emerging, she felt like Alice, for here was Wonderland, the perfect pool: turquoise water set in white rock, fed by a waterfall; on the side of the wadi wall there were rocky ledges and boulders dressed in maidenhair fern to jump from, and between the reeds and the water, dry gravelly strands to lie on. The pool was inhabited. Half a dozen Arab boys, Zara's age, stared at her silently as she

slid into the clearing, and w
her. She felt she ought to ask
its refusal. Stripping to her su
clothes onto the gravel and dived
was frigid. She swam the length of
got out, gasping.

The Arab boys had not moved, st          . She
said *"Shalom"* shyly, not looking at a            nd, after a
moment, one of them, a tall, curly-haired boy with startling
blue eyes in a dark face, answered politely, *"Ahalan."* With
that, the others turned from her and resumed a game of
follow-the-leader.

The leader was the blue-eyed boy who lead a series of
dives from a rock six feet above the water. The dives grew
more difficult, and Zara, watching, wished they'd let her
try; but she was ignored. Finally the leader got out of the
pool and climbed, not to the rock they'd been diving from
but to a higher one, ten feet above the pool, and with less of
an overhang than the ledge below it, so that a diver would
have to push off sharply and dive at an angle to miss it.
Seeing him hesitate, it occurred to Zara that he was showing
off for her, that the dive was not one he would otherwise
attempt. She felt angry and wanted to say something to stop
him. But the boy never glanced at her, and fear of
presumption captured her voice. He dived. One moment
he'd stood tense and thoughtful on the edge of the rock, the
next his arms were breaking water and his body following,
sliding smooth as an otter into the pool. His dive carried
him to the bottom of the pool, and there it flattened out,
skimming inches above the ground. Zara throbbed with
admiration and envy. And decided: no matter how long she
had to stay, she was going to wait till these boys left, then
do that dive herself.

...er hour they left, and she did, after gathering ...ge with several practice dives from the lower ledge. Climbing onto the rock, she looked down carefully, then backed off. A few running steps, and she launched herself up and out with an inarticulate shout or invocation. Her body jackknifed and entered the water in a shallow dive that, nevertheless, took her to the bottom and all the way across the pool underwater. Zara rose on the far side of the pool crowing with delight. It made it even better, she thought a bit wistfully, that no one had seen. A perfect act needs no witnesses. Then a witness stepped forth, from the shelter of the reeds. "Not bad," said the blue-eyed boy, "for a girl."

"Neither was yours, for an Arab," she instantly replied and feared, as he looked sharply at her, that she'd gone too far. But no, he smiled, then he laughed, and Zara joined in. That was Raif.

But the next time she saw Raif, he refused to speak to her. She was with the Betar group then, which Micha had persuaded her to join. After the initial teasing, he'd begun walking home from school with her. It wasn't, he explained, that he saw much use in girls, but he figured that the only two Ashkenazim in their class ought to stick together.

"The only two what?" Zara echoed blankly.

"Ashkenazim," Micha repeated. "All the others are Sephardim. Didn't you know that?"

"What's the difference?"

"Don't you know anything, Zara? Ashkenazim come from Europe and Russia, Sephardim are from the East."

"I'm from America."

"Doesn't matter; it goes by your parents. Yours are *Yekkes*, Germans."

slid into the clearing, and waited to see who would follow her. She felt she ought to ask permission but couldn't risk its refusal. Stripping to her suit, Zara dropped her school clothes onto the gravel and dived into the pool. The water was frigid. She swam the length of the pool and back, then got out, gasping.

The Arab boys had not moved, still watching her. She said "*Shalom*" shyly, not looking at anyone and, after a moment, one of them, a tall, curly-haired boy with startling blue eyes in a dark face, answered politely, "*Ahalan.*" With that, the others turned from her and resumed a game of follow-the-leader.

The leader was the blue-eyed boy who lead a series of dives from a rock six feet above the water. The dives grew more difficult, and Zara, watching, wished they'd let her try; but she was ignored. Finally the leader got out of the pool and climbed, not to the rock they'd been diving from but to a higher one, ten feet above the pool, and with less of an overhang than the ledge below it, so that a diver would have to push off sharply and dive at an angle to miss it. Seeing him hesitate, it occurred to Zara that he was showing off for her, that the dive was not one he would otherwise attempt. She felt angry and wanted to say something to stop him. But the boy never glanced at her, and fear of presumption captured her voice. He dived. One moment he'd stood tense and thoughtful on the edge of the rock, the next his arms were breaking water and his body following, sliding smooth as an otter into the pool. His dive carried him to the bottom of the pool, and there it flattened out, skimming inches above the ground. Zara throbbed with admiration and envy. And decided: no matter how long she had to stay, she was going to wait till these boys left, then do that dive herself.

In another hour they left, and she did, after gathering courage with several practice dives from the lower ledge. Climbing onto the rock, she looked down carefully, then backed off. A few running steps, and she launched herself up and out with an inarticulate shout or invocation. Her body jackknifed and entered the water in a shallow dive that, nevertheless, took her to the bottom and all the way across the pool underwater. Zara rose on the far side of the pool crowing with delight. It made it even better, she thought a bit wistfully, that no one had seen. A perfect act needs no witnesses. Then a witness stepped forth, from the shelter of the reeds. "Not bad," said the blue-eyed boy, "for a girl."

"Neither was yours, for an Arab," she instantly replied and feared, as he looked sharply at her, that she'd gone too far. But no, he smiled, then he laughed, and Zara joined in. That was Raif.

But the next time she saw Raif, he refused to speak to her. She was with the Betar group then, which Micha had persuaded her to join. After the initial teasing, he'd begun walking home from school with her. It wasn't, he explained, that he saw much use in girls, but he figured that the only two Ashkenazim in their class ought to stick together.

"The only two what?" Zara echoed blankly.

"Ashkenazim," Micha repeated. "All the others are Sephardim. Didn't you know that?"

"What's the difference?"

"Don't you know anything, Zara? Ashkenazim come from Europe and Russia, Sephardim are from the East."

"I'm from America."

"Doesn't matter; it goes by your parents. Yours are *Yekkes*, Germans."

"So?"

"So Ashkenazim are different. We're better at stuff like reading and thinking and we've got culture. The Sephardim are more like Arabs."

"Oh," she said, having come to the boundaries of acceptable ignorance. But Micha, enjoying the role of initiator, went on kindly.

"See, it's a natural thing; it's in our genes. Like girls are better than boys at stuff like sewing and cooking, and boys are better at running and swimming."

Zara stopped walking and faced him, body belligerent, eyes green ice. "I wouldn't sew a stitch to save my life, and I'll bet anything I'm a better swimmer than you."

Micha just laughed delightedly, like a boy whose pet monkey has just displayed untaught tricks. "Think you're one of the boys, Zara?"

"No, I'm one of the girls," she retorted, and turned to stalk off.

But Micha stretched out an arm and caught her by the wrist, holding tight. Zara kept turning as though trying ineffectually, girlishly, to pull free. Then, as he shifted backward to counterbalance, she suddenly reversed direction and swung around, driving her free fist with all her force into his stomach. He let go and staggered back, face blank with astonishment. Zara ran home.

She was sure he would hate her for that trick, but the next day in school he was friendly and ostentatiously respectful. When, on the same day, two kids and a teacher asked her to join the Betar youth group of which Micha was a leader, Zara sensed he was behind it and promised to think it over.

She reasoned that if he didn't hate her for punching him, he was a possible friend and therefore not to be taken lightly. Ruth, when Zara told her of the invitation, was unexpectedly enthusiastic. Those groups believe in self-reliance and strength, she said, and Jews should learn such things from childhood. But Zara still shrank from the idea. Once, giving into her mother, Zara had joined the Girl Scouts and found the activities stupid and the meetings a terrible waste of her precious private time. Why join the youth group when she could use the same time to run free? Besides, she didn't like Weisburger, the group leader.

Weisburger taught them modern and biblical history, and interspersed his lectures with jokes and stories mocking the Arab mentality, calling it cowardly, stupid, and primitive. The kids liked him because he was so easy to distract from the assigned material: all that was necessary was to introduce some Arab question and he was off, drenching his words in an excess of saliva. Zara the foreigner had no knowledge with which to contest him on his own ground, but she recognized the spirit. She'd known his type in New York: a hater with wily ways. He addressed her in insultingly simple Hebrew, praised her personally for "coming up to the Land" ("Marlboro Country," she would finish silently), and said that her parents had "political maturity." Zara thought that sounded horrible, maybe fatal, and rudely said that she hoped it wasn't catching. All the kids laughed at her first joke in Hebrew. But Weisburger didn't find it funny, and unlike Micha he bore grudges. Zara felt that most of all he disliked her for the very thing he praised: that she, a foreigner, had come to his land. And it was strange that she felt this, because in fact Israel was not his country: his country was Poland, which he had left as a full-grown man.

Such a puny man, with sparse reddish hair and thick tinted glasses and skin so pale that he had always to wear a wide straw hat to protect himself outside! Later he would return to Zara's dreams, the embodiment of a hated spirit in her land, this frailish Pied Piper leading troops of sturdy dark children, in chants and anthems, singing "The Land is ours, the Land is ours," while the Land was so much not his that he had to wear absurd hats and dark glasses to block out the Land's essence, its pure light.

On such a march was Zara lead by Weisburger, when at last she let her mother push and Micha pull her into joining Betar; down the hill, across the wadi, and up into the Arab village, Dar Ayun, singing marching rhythms: "The Land Is Ours" and "The People of Israel Live!" and Zara, starting out to make the best of it, and now for the first time in her life feeling part of a group, sang along lustily as they marched. She hardly noticed the coldness of the Arab villagers, who stared sullenly, unlike the Jews who'd cheered the unruly parade. She sang out and kicked dust with her sandaled feet, swung her arms and competed for position near the front with the strong walkers. Then they came opposite the Arab school and, among the mass of children who stood silently in the yard, she saw Raif.

Zara yelled out his name and waved, thrilled that he should see her in a parade. He seemed to see her but must not have, since he didn't wave back.

"Raif!" she called again and darted out of line toward him. Then Raif passed through the mob of children as gracefully as he cut through water and came to stand between her and them. Just as he reached her, Zara's shoulder was wrenched painfully from behind, and she knew before turning that it must be Weisburger. He was furious, but seemed curiously frightened as well, his eyes darting from her to Raif and the other Arab kids. "Get back in line," he hissed. Zara looked at Raif, but his face was utterly closed to her, and he said, "Get out of here."

The whole youth group had halted and seen. Unable to
look at them, she felt them staring at her, despising her for
her ignorance and stupidity. She remembered all of Weisburger's Arab jokes and knew that now she was tarred
forever with the same brush. Weisburger shook her again,
roughly, and said in a high voice, "Get back in line."

"No!" Zara screamed, and bent back his finger to break
his grip on her. She ran down the street, blond hair flying
behind, a long-legged palomino filly; and those who looked
after her felt weighty and earthbound, incapable of pursuit.

She ran back to Tivon, but not home. Not home, where
Ruth's smothering sympathy would ooze over her, coating
her in more than motherly concern. Home was not the place
to bring her wounds, where Ruth would see them, salve
them, and then use them.

Two partners were in that love relation: Ruth, whose
focus was narrow but whose beam was intense and who
loved with flagrant disregard of boundaries; and Hope,
whose love was as defensive as Ruth's was invasive. Once,
Ruth's touch had been all that held Hope in existence:
without it she would have dissolved. This was the result of a
misunderstanding so basic that it nearly invalidated Hope's
world.

Her parents were survivors of Buchenwald and Auschwitz. Rational people, they decided not to tell their child
about the Holocaust until she had gained some counterbal-
ancing American experience of her own. But, as children
learn what their parents are before they are capable of
understanding what they say, so Hope imbibed her mother's
reality with her mother's milk and found no more to wonder
at in the one than in the other. Since both her parents had
tattooed numbers on their arms, Hope classified it before
she could speak of it as an attribute of adulthood.

Ruth and Henry jealously guarded their child at home while other parents in the neighborhood were forming play groups and registering for nursery schools. But they knew that normal American children must attend kindergarten; and when Hope reached five, her mother, unsuccessfully trying to hide her distress, led her to school and left her there. All went well on the first day until the teacher, Joanne, distributed toys randomly from a toy chest, and Hope drew a shiny, red fire engine. This so infuriated one little boy that he grabbed the toy, shouting, "Fire engines are for boys!" and smote the presumptuous female in the head with it. Hope clutched her head and cried, but when Joanne rushed over to hug and comfort her, the child's cries choked off abruptly, as though she'd quit breathing. Joanne looked down and saw that the child was staring at her arms, bare on the hot Indian summer day, with a look of puzzled concentration that slowly changed to fear. Clutching Joanne's arm she vigorously rubbed a spot on her forearm, then examined the place she had rubbed. Nothing showed through. Hope screamed: not a whine or a shriek but the lusty help-seeking cry of a child in serious trouble. Joanne was unable to comfort her. Hope's mother was sent for.

Ruth's beeline dash for her child was so indistractible that any child in her way would have been trampled. But her daughter was hardly in her arms before she began apologizing to the teacher. "I'm so sorry; she's a good child, she doesn't cause problems." She takes up no room, she doesn't eat much, spare her.

"Mommy, look at her arms," Hope shrilled accusingly from the safety of her mother's embrace. Joanne's bewilderment as she reexamined her inoffensive arms was apparent, but Ruth, after just one glance, grew a shade paler.

"Nothing is wrong with her arms," she said in the firmest tone she had ever used to her daughter.

"But they're empty, Mommy. Where's her number? How can she take care of us if she has no number?"

Ruth had covered her arms, but couldn't get rid of her accent. Not so many years had passed since the end of the war. Comprehension, horror, pity, and shame combined to trap Joanne's tongue, while Ruth hugged her child tightly and stared at the floor. The kindergarten children had no difficulty filling the silence. "Crybaby," they whispered audibly, and one slightly bolder child pronounced: "She's crazy. She thinks grown-ups have numbers. What a loony!" They would, Ruth knew, go home and tell their mothers.

Realizing that some grave error had crept into her concept of the world, but unable to trace its source, Hope saw blackness and her mother's face, felt nothing but coldness and those parts where her mother's warming touch made her exist. Ruth had to carry her daughter home.

When reality crumbles, a lifeline is necessary. Hope's young world reassembled naturally, but Ruth's blast had been irreversible. The balance of need had shifted. As Ruth's child, seeming to absorb energy directly from the Mediterranean sun, grew into not tallness but the impression of it, as her eyes turned their focus outward and her body gained strength and confidence, did Ruth rejoice? She would have if she could.

But a dream came to Ruth when they first settled in Tivon, and returned remorselessly, forcing her to experience nightly Hope's leaving her. Not gradually, like other people's children, but a sudden, total, irrevocable split. And in the dream, all her efforts to prevent this disaster serve only to bring it on. Hope the baby, Hope the child, Hope the treacherous, now showing wavering outlines of womanhood, now answering to her true mother-given name only as a kindness: must Ruth rejoice in her daughter's growing capacity to destroy her?

And sensing her coming obsolescence in her daughter's life, did Ruth fight it? She did indeed, indeed she did. The old cosmological bond, Jews against the world, the cowboys-and-Indians, Nazi-Jew axis had failed her, lost its bonding power in the country where they were the ruling class. A new conception had to replace it, to fulfill its function. Ruth's vision narrowed and intensified: in place of Jews against the world, the new credo was family against the world. A not indefensible position, with Ruth's remembered treacheries, treacherous memories. Hope, growing out of her mother's shadow, may have recognized the stratagems, but did recognition immunize? Her mother's whispered message, in all its forms, penetrated to the core of Zara, for only Ruth knew the soft, secret entrances still left in the hardening chrysalis. The message was: "No friend will ever care about you as your family cares. When you need help, only your family will be there to give it. Trust no one. Loyalty resides in the family."

Sometimes Hope tried reason. "But if you can't trust anyone outside the family, Mother, then how do new families get started? How can you marry if no outsider can be trusted?"

"You marry for survival, because it's worse to stay alone, and you marry to have children. But no bond between man and woman has the strength of the bond between mother and child."

And father and child? Hope wondered, hurt by her mother's exclusion of her father; but this thought she never spoke aloud.

Accepting comfort now from Ruth meant joining her in

exile. "We are strangers in a strange land and must cleave together"; those were the terms of Ruth's sympathy. If she could get out of paying, Zara would.

After bolting Betar, Zara ran to Rachamim, her teacher and friend. Entering his home at this moment meant opening one final door as a hundred others slammed in her face. She had distrusted him for a long time because she knew he'd been set on her: Sic her, they'd told him, you're the class counselor. Integrate that little foreign girl; move her along with her social problems. And Rachamim, seeing the fog of disapproval around her grow denser, nearly visible, seeing the tight net of unanimous small-town judgment (never stated, communicated by a look, a silence, a tone, to themselves and to her) float softly down to entrap her, had known it was time for some intervention and accepted the call. He understood villages, but she was from a city, unaware of her danger. Freedom cried out for interference, and if he didn't try, then surely someone else would step on this pretty little butterfly's wings. Besides, he liked her, saw through her distrust of him and everyone, to the stoicism under fire which they called sullenness. So many of the kids he saw were already, by nine or ten years old, little replicas of their parents, predetermined form and content, appearing integral. Zara was still very much incomplete, awkward, branches shooting off her in all directions, and though there was no telling which would flower, which atrophy, already there were elements to her, strength and a promise of grace, that drew him to her.

He'd arranged for her to study Arabic, while her class had English, and received for that favor thanks but no softening. He'd showed her where his house was and said the door was open, and Zara had looked suspiciously at him. But after the Betar fiasco, unwilling to go home, she came to Rachamim's door. When he first saw her, he frowned, and Zara pulsed with the unexpected pain of this final rejection. But then she saw that he was frowning at her uniform, not her. He looked at her face, grimaced sympathetically, as if he knew how they'd wedged her into it, and opened the door.

He listened closely to her story, stammered out in lapsing Hebrew, then told her: "The mistake isn't yours, Zara. Those who are secure in their place here have no need to march past their neighbors' homes shouting absurdities about ownership. The Bedouin of the Sinai, and the few outsiders who've learned their ways, walk through the desert wilderness where no other men can survive. They wear long robes to preserve water, and they know how to cope with constant heat and wind. I don't want to romanticize them, they are themselves the least sentimental people in the world. I only mean to show that if any people has a sensible claim to ownership of land, it's the desert Bedouin. But they never do claim ownership because those with the strongest claim have the least need to proclaim it."

But Rachamim's approval meant nothing to Zara's classmates, who knew her now as an Arab-lover. Unrepentant Zara needed punishing, but she was hard to get at. It was Weisburger who finally showed the way.

The lesson was on the Holocaust. Weisburger listed on the blackboard the countries of Europe, followed by two columns of numbers: their Jewish population before and after the war.

"Six million died," he said. "Everybody knows that number. But what does it mean? It's as if every Jew in this country were to be killed—twice. And even those few European Jews who escaped death didn't escape destruction: they survived as orphans, widows, homeless casta-

ways. Most of you, or your parents, come from Arab lands.
But these European Jews, they were your cousins, your kin.
We have in our village a new family that suffered directly
and personally under the Nazi regime. Tikva, where did
your parents pass the war?"

She'd been window-gazing. Now she looked at him and
shook her head once, warningly. He looked stern and said,
"Stand up."

Reluctantly, she stood.

"I'll ask again. Where were your parents during the
war?"

It was no right of his to overrule her mother's enjoined
silence. But a third time he asked and forced her to answer:
"Auschwitz. Buchenwald."

The names brought a gust of evil into the room and all of
it attached to Zara. Helplessly, she felt the embarrassment
of her classmates congeal into hostility. Weisburger pushed
on.

"Where is the rest of your family?"

Understanding now what he was doing and feeling it to
be wholly malicious, she compressed her lips and would not
speak.

"Where are your grandparents, your uncles and aunts,
your cousins?"

The room was full of whispers, all about her. Impassively Zara pulled her knapsack from under her desk.
"Speak up, girl, answer the question. Tikva, where do you
think you're going?"

She was at the door. She needed all her mother's strength
to keep her voice steady as she answered: "Mind your own
business, you dirty leech." Then she went out, closing the
door on the uproar behind her.

At recess they got her. Six of them came over to where

she sat reading over her Arabic lesson. "Where's your Grandma?" Uri asked sweetly. She stood up and pivoted, but Moshe was behind her, blocking the way. "Where's your Grandpa?" he asked. They formed a circle around her; any watching teacher would take this for a game. "Where are your uncles, Zara? Where are your aunts? Where are your cousins, and what do they do? What did your daddy do during the war, Zara?" Where was Micha, that was her question; where was he when she needed him? Out of sight. She shoved Moshe experimentally but the circle held.

"Where's your Grandma; where's your Grandpa?" They were chanting it now. She could see this going on for a long time. Her refusal to cry fed their anger. Uri stepped into the circle and pushed his face up to hers. Garlic breath. "You come from a family of yellow-bellied cowards," he told her. "My father says the German Jews were too scared to fight. How come they just lined up for the slaughter, Zara? People like that don't belong here. You're sheep, and we're wolves. The Arabs give us grief, we just wipe them out. Israelis aren't afraid to fight. Why don't you go back where you belong?" She kicked his knee as hard as she could, and as his friends reached to steady him she escaped. But not far. Ten yards away, her back safely to a wall, she filled her hands with rocks and shrieked:

"You want to fight? I'm not afraid. One at a time, or all together. Come on, who's scared now, come you goddamn Nazis, come on you—" she stopped as Weisburger suddenly loomed over her.

"What did you say?" Voice low but excited, eyes wide with fulfilled expectation. Oh he'd been waiting for this.

"Leave me alone."

"Oh no. Oh no. I heard what you said. If you dare—if I ever hear those words again, I'll have your parents down here so fast you won't know what hit you. How'd you like them to find out about this?" She was backing away, keeping a wary eye on her gaping classmates. His voice bellowed after her. "That's one word I won't tolerate, and coming from you of all people—" Out of reach, she stopped and shouted back: "If they act like Nazis, I'll call them Nazis. I'm not afraid of you!" Then, prudently, she ran.

Though the hillside where she walked was noon-still and summer bright, though a light breeze rustled through the dry brush, Zara was back in a dark room in her parents' New York apartment, listening to her mother's voice, learning her mother's lesson.

On her seventh birthday, the children in school asked her what present her grandparents had given her. She lied and said, "a bicycle." Later she walked home from school, hand in hand with her mother. Hope was preoccupied, and Ruth, sensitive to her mood, did not speak. Only when the apartment door was safely latched behind them did Hope break her silence and ask, "Do I have grandparents?"

Ruth looked into her daughter's face. "Did they ask you that, the children?"

Hope looked down.

For a moment, Ruth was still. Then she nodded once, decisively, and said, "Come here." She didn't wait for Hope to follow, but marched her along in front, into the living room. She unlocked the cupboard forbidden to Hope and drew out a dusty, leather-bound photograph album. "Sit down. You're old enough now to know your family." If that was so, then whence Hope's sudden indisposition to know? But it was too late; questions asked were irrevocable and that's why, in the family, they were rarely spoken.

Hope knelt in her father's large chair and craned to see the album laid out on the desk. Ruth stood behind her. Hope was chilled by her mother's strained, rasping voice even as she was warmed and comforted by the gentle warmth of Ruth's hands on her shoulders.

"Open the book."

The first page was blank. Hope twisted to look into her mother's face, but Ruth kept her eyes on the album. "My mother, your grandmother. Now turn the page."

She did. Blank again. "Your grandfather," said Ruth. "Next."

Blank. "Your Aunt Elsa—my little sister. Go on."

"Your Uncle Peter. Turn."

"Your—cousin." For the first time Ruth's voice faltered, but she went on: "David, I think. Elsa always liked that name."

They were all there, uncles, aunts, grandparents, cousins, and second cousins, the dead and the unborn. All those blank pages, and her mother's shadow on them, and her harsh voice and gentle hands, and the desperate forbidden questions fighting to come out. But Hope resisted, as she knew she must. Her mother's pain laid an awful charge on her: to protect Ruth forever from further pain. What matter those fearful mysteries burning inside her, compared to that solemn charge? Closing the album, Hope sniffled like a child hurt but trying hard to deny it. Ruth encouraged stoicism by comforting unacknowledged wounds while ignoring flaunted ones. Now she kissed Hope tenderly and rocked her and whispered in her ear: "I had to show you so you'd know one thing. The only people you have—the only people in the world who care for you—are your father and mother."

How clearly Zara had learned the truth of her mother's words. Yet she could not bear the sting of acknowledging their truth once again, and she could hide nothing from

Ruth. Without conscious direction, her legs had carried her down into the wadi, and she found herself close to the hidden pool. Praying, as best she could without practice, that the pool would be deserted, she crawled through the passage. It was. She knew things she was never meant to know; if only she could drown the knowledge without drowning herself.

Weisburger's sour breath clung to her face, and her clothes were soiled with the taunts of her classmates. Fully dressed, she lay in the cold water, resting her head on the bank. With her eyes closed, she could feel the sun drawing the poison from her. Here was a safe place to cry in. Her stomach began to heave, drawing air in hoarse sharp gasps. Her chest and throat constricted around dry rhythmic sobs. The tears reached her eyes and overflowed, but that was the least of it. When it was over, her stomach ached but she felt extraordinarily well and peaceful.

Suddenly aware of a presence, she turned and saw Raif. What grave eyes he had, for all their surprising blueness.

She was furious. She never would have cried before witnesses, hadn't since she was old enough to control herself. But when he turned to go, she remembered what she owed him and called: "Raif!"

He stopped and looked at her. "Wait," she said, crawling onto the dry stand. "I have to tell you something."

He sat beside her and didn't seem to mind her sopping school clothes dripping onto his khaki pants. Zara said, "I'm sorry I came with those Betar jerks. It was a mistake."

He nodded. "You're new around here, aren't you?"

"Yeah."

He said gently, "We don't like it, you know, when they come marching through our village like they own it, singing that stupid song."

"I understand. I'd hate them."

"I don't hate them but it's dumb, like rubbing salt into a wound. What does it get them?"

"They're like that. They like rubbing salt into wounds. You should hate them. I do."

Puzzled, Raif said, "Well, you're one of them, aren't you?"

Question or accusation? She squinted at him and decided on the former. She answered, "Not really," and explained why. After that, it seemed there was a lot to talk about. Somehow they got onto schools and teachers, and she discovered that he knew Rachamim and had been to his house several times. Weisburger of course he knew. Whenever the Betar group marched through Dar Ayun, he told her, little kids spread the word: "Here come the albino mule and his marching ass band!"

Oh it was good to laugh at Weisburger. Indeed laughter was the only thing that helped, and she was grateful to Raif for showing her that.

Evening seemed to take a great leap forward that day. Before they were half done talking, twilight fell, and Zara had to go.

It was as if the making of a friend had to be paid for by the deepening of enmities. When Raif's mates found out that he was friendly with a Jewish girl, they beat him. Raif wouldn't tell her that, but Daud, Raif's best friend, did. He'd resented Zara at first but came around when she offered to fight him. He'd looked at her carefully then. She had no breasts to speak of; she was as tall as he was and stringy and strong as a half-grown mountain lion. He figured it was okay to accept. Zara fought dirty but not girlishly; when he won he felt he'd earned the victory. He pulled her up and offered her his hand.

Zara had a rigid sense of what was due a freely chosen friend, and Raif's absence from her school life was no excuse for shirking. Particularly since he wasn't there, she had to take his side. But whenever she resisted, whenever she questioned the Zionist catechism, censure flew to her like lightning to a pine in a grove of gnarled olive trees.

"Zionism," Weisburger explained one day, fanning himself—he hadn't the knack of sweating healthily, and so sweltered through the endless summers, weak, irritable, and prone to headache—"Zionism is a living movement which will not be fully realized until every Jew is an Israeli, and every Israeli a Jew."

"What will you do to the Israeli Arabs?" piped the voice he'd grown to hate. Some of her classmates giggled; others groaned, "Not again, Zara." Even Micha made a face. But she was convinced that hers was the voice of reason —Raif's voice.

Raif had a philosophy—no, not a philosophy but a single, passionate tenet. People should control their lives. To do so meant eliminating or reducing the effect of accident. Birth—race, religion, class even—sex were accidental factors and so as far as possible were to be ignored. He and Zara speculated endlessly about how far they could apply his principle in reality. When Daud was with them, the discussion invariably turned to argument. "Raif's grand delusion," Daud called it.

Once, when the three of them were stealing apples from an orchard on the edge of Tivon, Daud and Raif climbed the same tree. Soon the branches were shaking and the leaves flying with the force of their whispered argument, while

Zara, picking in the next row, kept a sharp eye out for villagers.

"If this one principle," said Raif, "were applied as a test to all the laws of this country, you'd have your secular democratic state, including the right of return for exiled Palestinians." Daud answered:

"If you think race doesn't matter and religion doesn't count, buddy, you better get off of that cloud before you take a fall. Because how're you going to make it stick? I say the world's flat and I get a hundred people to agree with me: does that make it flat?"

Raif laughed and said, "Why not, you flathead?"

"If fools could fly, man, you'd be bound for the moon."

"Calling me a fool?" and there followed a flurry of apples.

Uzi Cohen, whose orchard it was, was amazed to find that single tree stripped bare the next day, and apples strewn around it. Some crazy kind of dust-devil, he decided at last, and went about his work.

They taught her things, these Arabs did, that weren't on the program; and Zara never minded the trouble it caused. Wasn't there, in fact, something very right about her isolation, some hidden truth to it? Ruth thought there was. For though she encouraged Zara to join in group activities, she was secretly proud of her daughter's aloofness. For if Ruth's ordeal had any meaning, it was as a rite of selection: survival was akin to anointment and that made Hope the daughter of royalty. Why should Hope feel at home in this community of sweat-stained potato grubbers? Ruth did not. She was what the local children called her: the Queen of Spades. Oh but she did not mean for Hope to run with Arabs. No, that she would not have.

One day Zara came home from school hours late. In the dark salon she laid her head against her mother's cool hand.

"Where were you?" asked Ruth.

"I went to the wadi."

"Alone?"

Surprised, Zara answered smoothly, "I went alone. Do you think I'd go anywhere with those creeps from school?" She went alone to meet her friends. Those who called her sly were unfair; wasn't it her duty to protect her mother from pain and worry? But rumor's osmotic force had penetrated even their stone walls; Ruth knew.

"Tell me about your friends," she ordered quietly, and Zara, grateful for this seeming dispensation, was happy to obey.

"My best friend is Raif, but after him I like Daud. Daud is almost too good-looking, and he knows it, but Raif has more in him. Raif's a real good diver. Daud can do most of the same stuff but he does it because Raif does; Raif does it for love, and oh, Mommy, you should see him dive from the rocks. Rachamim says Raif has grace. At first I thought that was a soppy thing for a boy to have, but after a while I saw what he meant: it's not only in his body and the way he moves, it's in his mind. Like when the other boys laugh at my Arabic and make fun of my accent, Raif takes my side in a way that doesn't make them mad. He brings me kids' books in Arabic to help me with my reading—"

"Hope. You cannot be friends with an Arab."

Zara was aghast. Her mother had always been the keeper of the truth, the border guard on the boundary of the possible and the impossible. And yet she knew, as sure as the sun shone and the wadi sheltered, that Raif was her friend.

"But I am," she cried.

"It may seem so, but it's impossible."

Zara withdrew her hand from her mother's and rubbed it to restore the warmth. She had erred; she had mixed up her worlds and now there was danger of drawing Ruth's black star out of its proper firmament and into Raif's constellation. She had no power over Ruth. To argue was absurd, like trying to talk the sun into backtracking; still she said hopelessly:

"You don't know him," and Ruth, inevitably, replied:

"I don't need to."

"He doesn't care that I'm a Jew."

"He doesn't have to act like an enemy to be one."

"He doesn't hate. He can't. He tells me I should make peace with the kids at school. He's a pacifist." Too late she remembered Ruth's contempt for pacifists.

"He's a wolf in sheep's clothing, and you're a foolish little Red Riding Hood. Listen to me, Hope." She had to strain to obey, for Ruth's voice had dropped ominously. "Stay out of the wadi."

Zara's silent misery was not unfelt by Ruth. Insofar as she could separate her daughter from herself, she loved Hope. But she did not soften; Ruth's love was made of steel.

After a while Zara said, "I'll bring him to you. You'll talk to him, and then you'll like him."

"Nothing he could say would make a difference."

"Why not? Don't ideas matter? Raif makes more sense than anything I've learned at school."

"Let me hear some of these ideas."

Now Zara was unwilling, but trapped. She said:

"He thinks we should control our lives, that the accident of where and what and when we were born shouldn't determine who we are or how we think."

"Race doesn't matter?" Ruth repeated incredulously; even in the dim light Zara could see her mother's face darken dangerously. "Religion doesn't matter?"

"Shouldn't," she corrected nervously.

"Shouldn't?" and the word turned to venom in her mouth. "That's a fine word, a fine moral word. Only 'shouldn't' has no place in my house." This was disaster, yet something in Zara rejoiced. Was it at the reemergence of the old Ruth, the transcendent Ruth? This Ruth's anger was not her own, but others'; this Ruth's world was one of mythic proportion, in which her suffering was containable, her survival endurable. For Zara, who had since childhood shuttled regularly between her mother's and the outer world, there was nothing outlandish in this shift of context.

"The Nazis," said Ruth, giving each word the weight of gospel, "erased 'shouldn't' from the language. Now it's a fantasy word, fit for idiots and children; and no child of mine—do you hear, Hope?—no child of mine is entitled to such idiocy."

Dry-eyed, silent, and outwardly subdued, Zara secretly determined to show greater consideration by employing greater stealth.

Zara's only school friend was Micha, whose status as undisputed leader of their class allowed him a degree of eccentricity; handsome Micha, only son of a Russian widow, treated as the man of the house since the age of six when his mother's friendship with an important bureaucrat brought them a visa and a ticket to Israel. His father he hardly remembered, but knew he had fought for the right to emigrate, been declared a Zionist gangster, arrested and sentenced to nine years in Siberia, where he died. From his mother, Micha learned the value of making the right friends, and from the legacy of his father he took a warning against adopting the wrong stance at the wrong time in the wrong place. His inheritance set his boundaries, which he mocked but observed; but the noninherited, self-engendered essence of the boy was a clear, intense concentration, a joyous and intelligent curiosity that illuminated its own objects. When his focused gaze lit upon Zara, she felt warmth in her cold, shadowed parts, her mother's domain, where not even the Mediterannean sun penetrated. And the weight of Micha's own family shackles was lightened by his love for her stubborn independence, her outrageous illusions of strength, and her loner's freedom which his own leadership role did not bestow. He tested her always, and tried hard to dominate her, but was better pleased when he lost than when he won. The terms of the friendship were these: Zara would not be drawn into his Betar activities, and Micha would refrain from implementing their judgment upon her. The covenant worked, and the strange alliance continued unchanged until they were sixteen years old. Then a purpose beyond the simple, playful testing of strength gradually permeated Micha's attempts at domination, and the touching of their bodies during horseplay produced a combustion of feeling as spontaneous and uncontrollable as when the sun ignited brush fires of August in the hills of Tivon.

As attraction sharpened into opposition, they fought and argued so bitterly that at times the friendship seemed dead. Differences, papered over by a decision to like, ripped open with the first pronged attack, spreading the argument into capillaries of ideas and politics; but the thrusting point of the quarrel was Micha's hatred of Zara's Arab friends.

Outside of her family and her teacher Rachamim, Zara had three friends, and Micha's demand that she sacrifice two for one seemed murderous to her, an enormity which he with his wide circle could not or would not grasp.

One day in the summer of her sixteenth birthday, Zara lay outstretched on a ledge above the wadi swimming hole, outflung hand tipped by Raif's, who lay like a dark mirror image at her side. Raif with delicate eyes tried to overlook the recent disturbing changes in Zara's body, while Daud, watching them from above, darkly noted their unconsciously attuned movements and wondered what part jealousy had to play in perfect friendship. Half a dozen other Arab boys were in the water or sunning on the rocks.

A red dragonfly flitted by Raif's head and settled on Zara's knee. Watching it, she said, "Isn't it strange that in all the time we've been friends you've never been to my house?"

This roused Raif. He opened his eyes and said simply, "You've never asked me."

"I guess that's because it's not really my home. It's my mother's."

"What does she have against me?"

"I hope she doesn't know I still see you. But if she does, she thinks you're my enemy."

Raif laughed and said, "Then may all your enemies be like me."

Daud, who'd been listening, put in: "She thinks a good Arab is a dead Arab."

"No! But she judges everything by what happened to her. She's convinced that Jews can't ever rely on the friendship of Gentiles."

"Is she religious?" Raif asked.

"Her? My mother's an atheist who hates God's guts." She was more, Zara thought (though loyalty forbade saying it); Ruth had a saboteur's measuring view of the kingdom of heaven and a righteous contempt for believers.

"And your father?"

"My father's a charitable man; he feels it's more charitable not to believe."

"Sometimes," interrupted Daud, "your mother makes sense to me. I accept Marx's view of religion as an opiate. It cuts the edge off a man. It's meant to."

Raif shrugged. "Meant by who? You think there's some secret conspiracy that meets every week to decide how to deal with Daud?"

"You think there's not?" challenged Daud, whose belief in conspiracy approached the spiritual.

"I think the whole religious thing's irrelevant. It's a matter of pure chance which religion you're born into, and whether you happen to draw the one true God out of all the false ones, *if* there is a true one. I wouldn't bet my belief on odds like—what's that?"

They fell silent, and heard footsteps approaching from the Tivon side and Hebrew-speaking voices. Suddenly the voices joined in song: the Betar anthem.

The boys in the water started climbing out, but Raif motioned for them to remain where they were. Then the bushes parted, and Micha pushed through, followed by Uri, Moshe, Gadi, and the rest of the boys from the Betar group. They wore the shirts of their Betar uniforms over bathing trunks.

Silence, a counting and sizing up. Then Zara said, "Hey, Micha. What brings you guys here?"

"Why shouldn't we be here? It's ours."

"Feel free," said Raif in Hebrew, with a negligent wave of his hand, a casual host.

"What do you mean, feel free?" Micha advanced, backed

by his troops. "This place is ours. The wadi is government land, leased to Tivon. It's you guys who need permission." Though he spoke to Raif, his eyes, less delicate than Raif's, toured Zara's body.

Raif stood up. He was on higher ground than Micha, but the two boys were nearly the same size. Zara, still reclining, felt a sensual pleasure in their confrontation that she wouldn't identify, but pretended was merely aesthetic. The composition might have been entitled, "Different Racial Types Under Mediterranean Sun." Micha, son of Russian Jews, had wavy brown hair, hard green eyes, high cheekbones in a sculpted face. Raif wore an untamed crop of tight black curls over deep-set eyes in a brown face. Both their bodies were lean and broad-shouldered, containing graceful outlines of future maturity.

"Why don't you save yourself some trouble," Micha said kindly, "and just get out. We're using the hole today."

The boys in the pool drifted casually upward to form a group. As Zara joined their formation she said earnestly to Micha, "There's no reason for this. You've never wanted to swim here, but if you do now there's no reason why we can't all use it."

When he ignored her, and Raif did too, she understood at last that the capacity of the swimming hole to contain an increased volume of bodies was irrelevant. Micha whistled, and two more boys stepped into the clearing, holding a dozen stout sticks. "Unfair!" Zara started to cry out but stopped herself, knowing that further conversation with an armed opponent would be deemed cowardice.

Moshe, Micha's lieutenant, distributed the clubs among the Jewish boys. When Micha held his, he said to Raif, "Again—if you don't want to be beaten like dogs—get out."

Raif shrugged, and Daud spit. Micha sent his mocking smile into Raif's eyes. Offhandedly, he commanded, "Zara. Get out of here!"

She answered with an Arabic curse known to, but not generally used by, the Jewish kids. There was a rock near her right foot, and she scooped it up.

Stunned, Micha stared at her, then turned back tauntingly to Raif. "Cowards, letting a girl fight for you."

"I don't control her," the Arab answered. "She chooses for herself." A tenet of their joint religion. It infuriated Micha, who shouted, raised his stick, and charged Raif. At once a volley of rocks flew from the Arab side over Zara's head, into the group of rushing Jews. As Uri ran past her, Zara kicked out at his knee and he tripped, dropping his stick to break his fall. Zara caught it up. Micha was beating Raif with his stick, and the Arab boy, blocking some blows and absorbing others, was struggling to close in. Zara threw her rock with all her force and hit Micha's shoulder. As he swung around, Raif tackled him and brought him down. Zara ran over to where Daud lay on the ground, protecting his head while Moshe stabbed downward at his body with his club. She came up from behind, and swinging hard from the shoulder hit Moshe in the back. He fell over Daud, who immediately rolled on top and began punching.

Suddenly her hair was caught from behind, and her head snapped backward. Uri's reddened eyes stared madly into hers. She jabbed backward with her stick, but couldn't get any power into the backward swing, with the pain in her head and neck distracting her. "Dirty Arab-loving whore!" Uri screamed and raised his fist above her face. Before he could complete the blow, Raif jumped on his back with a cry of fury. Uri lost his balance but not his grip on Zara's hair. The three of them fell off the rock into the water below.

Uri got to his feet at once, but kept his grip on Zara's hair and held her head below the water. She struggled for the surface but couldn't overcome the strength of his arms; and in his eyes there was madness enough to teach her the fear of death. While her body fought on, her mind was engaged in a running review, not of her life but of her parents' rambling path toward Israel, toward safety, toward the place where their daughter was about to drown at the hand of a mad Jew. She pitied them. Suddenly, Raif was beside her, under the water, encouraging her with his eyes, while with both his hands he reached behind her head and grasped one of Uri's. She heard a sharp crack and then suddenly she was free, on her feet and sucking in air. Unable to control the trembling of her body, she leaned against Raif's supporting arm. She was surprised to see Micha near them in the water, but decided he must have come after Raif. Uri went on screaming, his hand cradled to his chest. The fighting had stopped.

Raif said in a voice sorrowful and wondering, "He tried to drown her. That Jew tried to drown a Jewish girl. What kind of animals are you?"

Micha's face was pinched and bloodless beneath his tan. He said, "I saw," and looked, just looked at Uri, who stopped crying and appeared frightened. Then he turned to Zara, and his eyes spoke an apology to her that he would not utter in front of the others. Zara had seen him in many conflicts on account of his feeling for her, but none so harsh as this wishing and not daring to speak. He settled it by saying, with menace in his voice and appeal in his eyes, "I'll talk to you later." Then he turned and strode out of the glade. The Jewish boys made way for him, and followed.

"Let me in, Zara."

"Fuck off. Take your hands off the door or I'll smash them." He did. She would.

He'd heard what Uri called her. A thousand beatings wouldn't put it out of their heads now. Only one way to save careless Zara now, by branding her himself. For her own salvation, not his pleasure. Nothing to do with the way she moved him, with the light behind her shining through her white blouse, silhouetting her legs, bare to her short-clad hips. Nothing to do with the sight of her, which only empowered him to do the act, her body the means, not the end. Her challenge to him since the day they'd met had only now revealed its natural arena, but this would not be just another skirmish. This action would mark the end of the war. Regrettable, yes, he gave her that much, but growing up he'd acquired the knowledge: colts have to be broken, girls have to be laid.

He didn't say, "I've come to save you." He serenaded her with his suffering, his dilemma, his striving for her, and her unwavering remoteness. "It was you I was after today, not them and not their filthy swimming hole. If you hate that way of reaching toward you, you must teach me another. You torment me and then blame me for reacting. Unfair, Zara!"

Knowing he was trying to invoke pity, she still pitied him.

Surely it was pity alone, and self-imposed obligation to even a former friend, that made her submit to his leading hand. It could not have been a recollection of the escalating excitement of other nighttime walks with him, nor the shamefully pleasurable suffusion she'd felt when Micha had crowed his challenge to Raif. Nor could any craven urge to resign herself into another's hands be admitted, to mar the pure charity of her concern for good old Micha.

In the orchard, Micha placed a tentative hand on her wrist and drew her down beside him.

"I came to apologize," he said handsomely and wove his fingers through her hair. When he touched the place that Uri had pulled, she flinched. Dispirited, his hand fell, but landed on her bare shoulder and found it still warm with absorbed sun. "But, Zara," voice lightening, fingers tightening, breath quickening, "it was your own fault."

"Mine?" she echoed, listening to his hand slide over her skin, wondering about the strange effect of moonlight on sun-infused bodies.

"You're not a child anymore, Zara." His hand for the first time touched the place that proved it so. Beneath the thin fabric of her blouse her breast was bare. She gasped; tension to and fro held her motionless. "You're my girl, always have been, and now's the time to realize it."

Her body signaled agreement by moving toward him. Then he said, "You don't belong with those Arabs anymore."

"Oh God," disgustedly. "Shut up."

He kissed her, thrusting his tongue in her mouth. This was teaching, this was true catechism, he saw it in a revelation; this is the only way women learn anything —physically, with perhaps some light verbal clarification thrown in.

They lay face to face. "I told them I'd kill anyone who touched you," Micha whispered. "I'd have murdered Uri if he hadn't already had a busted finger when I reached him. But he's out of Betar, for good."

She stiffened slightly and said, "Is that all you care about?

You came with clubs to beat up my friends, and you're just sorry I got hurt?"

"They've damn well got to learn to leave Jewish girls alone."

Suddenly Zara's body was a thrush in a trap, and Micha understood that he'd made a mistake; but the exquisite fluttering of her body held to his was more than he could give up. She was caught tight but her words flew against him. "Do Jewish girls have to learn to leave Arab boys alone? Is this your way of teaching me that? You will not make my choices for me, Micha."

"I love you," he said desperately. If love is the inability to let go, it was certainly true. "For God's sake, don't you understand that all they want from you is the chance to screw a Jewish girl?"

"And what do you want, Micha?"

"Not just sex."

"No—control, too." Twisting, she broke his grip on her with a trick he himself had taught her, fool that he was, and ran away.

# CHAPTER II

High school graduates entered the army together and finished in two groups, the girls after two years, the boys after three. The release every August of Tivon's sons and daughters was celebrated with a party in the high school auditorium. Another tradition held that engagements—long-standing or surprise—were announced during the party. Dozens of toasts were drunk by villagers unaccustomed to drinking; celebrants and mourners, winners and losers alike took part.

At twenty Zara finished her service in Nachal, the kibbutz-settling division of the army. She'd been stationed in Givat Shemesh for the year and a half following basic training, and the Galilee kibbutz had freed her nearly every weekend. The boys of the class were serving an additional year, but most had made it back for the party. One boy, Yair, was not expected. He'd been killed by a mine on a routine patrol in the desert. His parents had come, though, to wish the young girls well, and because ostensible mourning was disapproved of.

Zara came with her parents, but the others entered two by two, in colonizing pairs. Haya had a soldier boyfriend, uniformed, both of them looking proud as if he had already impregnated her. Miri had Uri, and they deserved each other. Orly led in an officer. And Micha, already wearing lieutenant's bars, was with Tsipi, the olive-skinned Moroccan beauty whom Zara had once envied. Her very demeanor as Micha's proud consort was a reproach to Zara's wanton ways, and there were plenty of looks to make her feel it.

Everyone knew whom Zara loved. He waited for her, down the hill and across the wadi.

People circulated, gravitated toward the buffet tables, and then settled in groups around tables. While they ate, an accordionist played. Every quarter of an hour, a glass would clink for silence, and the father of one of the girls (or a mother's brother, if there were no living father) made a short speech, competing for nonchalance. Orly's father gave a windy five-minute talk congratulating the girls for their valor in the face of the enemy, the enemy emerging as the would-be seducers they'd met while out of the protection of their own village, and saying that having paid their national dues, they were more fit than ever to take up the natural, true burdens of womanhood. "All honor to you!" he concluded, and drained his cup to enthusiastic applause. He sat down but got up immediately in response to his wife's look.

"My wife has reminded me to say that we'll expect you all at our place on September 9." He sat down again.

"What for, Yossi?" called a straight man.

Yossi looked surprised. "Didn't I mention it? Our Orly's marrying Yacov there, Captain Barash to all you privates."

Having with ill-concealed pity spoken all the necessary congratulations and received, instead of the customary *"B'karov etzlach"* (May it happen soon for you), just embarrassed thanks, Zara took time to lean against a wall and remember how she'd gone into the army.

She'd mentioned it first over a family supper of eggs, yoghurt, and salad one night. "In two months," she said conversationally, "I'll be drafted."

Ruth looked up slowly. She'd once had a kind of accusatory beauty, but now the accusation dominated. "Like hell you will."

Zara laughed, not unkindly. "They won't ask your permission, Mother. The state just takes me."

"I won't allow it."

"I'll be snatched from your very arms, Mother." This was the new link in the mother-daughter evolution, this choreographed combat on thin ice. Ruth had been dragged from her own mother's arms in the first selection upon entering Auschwitz, and her tubercular mother assigned to the gas chambers. Zara knew it and didn't: it had been one of her bedtime stories, but she'd forgotten them all. "But everybody's going. You should be glad that I'm finally in step."

"Don't be ridiculous. There could be a war. How do you think I would survive the anxiety if you were away when it started?"

"They don't send women to the front."

"The whole goddamn country's a front. Hope," Ruth's voice was steely, "you must say you're religious. They don't take religious girls."

"But I'm not."

"Then, Miss Scrupulous, say I am. It's enough that your family's religious to get out of it."

"Religious! You!"

Ruth bent across the table and stuck her furious face into Zara's. "What the hell do you think my religion is?"

Zara had some idea.

At the age of ten, she'd had a brief religious fling, brought on by a good religion teacher in school. One Friday night, Zara pled fatigue, went into her room and closed the door carefully behind her. She took two candlesticks from her school knapsack, and two candles. Ruth entered to find her standing with covered head bowed over the lighted candles, whispering the blessing. Ruth was appalled and frightened by the sound of that incantation, so bitterly and ironically recalled from her own childhood, issuing from her daughter's lips like a voice from the dead past. She rushed at Zara who, turning, threw up her hands as though she feared attack. But Ruth merely snatched the shawl from Zara's head and flung it, with the candles and candlesticks, out the window.

Fearing imminent retribution, Zara cried out. Ruth wheeled from the window and slapped her face. It was the first and only time she hit her daughter. It shocked them both, Zara into silence and Ruth into speech.

"It makes no sense," she said quietly, "with what you know of our family and our history, for you to bless God. It's treacherous. If he exists he's our enemy."

Then, seeing her daughter's eyes fill with unshed tears, she added, more softly still: "There's no hope in heaven. Only on earth." From somewhere the thought came to Zara that there's hope in hell too, if you live for retribution.

If Ruth had found a religion to fit the black hole of her renunciation, then God save Zara from the sight of it. She'd rather be drafted.

Surprisingly, Henry supported Zara. When Ruth informed him that they would leave the country if necessary to avoid the draft, he bellowed "No!" like a man insane. Ruth and Zara stared as he pounded the table and declared, "Never!"

Ruth's eyes sharpened on him like knives on a whetstone; with the blunt side of her voice she asked quietly, "Why not, Henry?"

"This is our home," he stammered. "We belong here."

"Oh, you feel at home here, Henry? You feel accepted? You've noticed how often they invite us to their homes, how they make us welcome?"

"Ruth, please."

"Stupid! We're lepers here! They take one look at these numbers and they turn away, despising us. To hell with them. I'm not giving them my daughter. Let them draft their own."

"Why do you separate everyone into us and them? We're all Jews here. Defending the country is defending ourselves."

"Big hero," Ruth sneered. "The man's so brave he's willing to send his daughter to fight! Go enlist yourself, hero."

Henry fled.

Ruth was a maniacal fighter, Zara thought, watching her warily. She knew no moderation: show her an opening and she'd drive a stake through it. Accusing Henry of cowardice was like twisting a knife in a festering wound: cruel but effective.

Ruth had never forgiven him for bringing them to Israel. He'd persuaded her by using Zara, claiming that her failure in school, her antisociability, were the results of her position as the child of survivors in an alien land. But she knew he had other reasons. For Ruth, the Holocaust was trauma, the crystallizing inner core of her life which patterned all subsequent experience. But for her husband, it was slow burning acid, an insult which took years to sink in fully, years to rankle, years finally to burn with the devouring acrid burn of unavenged malicious injury. His helplessness in America was that of the vagabond whose blinkered eyes are fixed on a single unattainable need, whose manhood, hostage to the past, is held for impossible ransom. He lusted to go back in time, to fight the bastards, to avenge his own passivity by dealing in death. He could not speak of it. Speaking, the gall of it would have burned his mouth; complaining or begging forgiveness for his irremediable shame would have added the venial sin of whining to the cardinal one of ineffectuality and destroyed the last remnants of his manhood.

Always a quiet man, through the years in New York he grew into a silent one. His clerical work required only occasional monosyllables, he made no friends, and his free hours were customarily spent in the company of his wife and daughter, who accepted him with or without speech. Occasionally, though, he would roam, leaving the apartment after dinner to walk through the city night, resting every few hours in an Automat or bar. He didn't drink. There were times when he could breathe and soothe the ache in his limbs only in the liquid medium of city anonymity, and could bear his own existence only if it went unnoticed by all around him.

The idea of Israel evolved slowly: he said he sought the security of a Jewish state, but Ruth knew he craved the danger of it. Redemption through risk, and it had worked for him; though his health was too poor for even the voracious Israeli army, they'd taken him into the civil guard and restored some of his pride. The government retrained him, and the light agricultural work which he was taught to do suited him better than office work. But Ruth had not thrived. And if he now thought to use her Hope as a step toward his redemption, she would soon teach him better. In this, though, Ruth had reckoned without Zara.

Fellow students ask baitingly if she wasn't being hypocritical, going to serve a country whose policies she despised. Her homespun political rationale ("You've got to guard the borders while the revolution goes on within") was considered a piece of characteristically arrogant provocation. Nor did her willingness to be drafted improve her standing among them: everyone had to go, so why not Zara? No points for nonshirking.

But it was Daud who took it worst, turning on her with a fury long denied expression. He put her on trial one night, in Rachamim's house, and cast himself as prosecutor. Daud was a spitfire talker with a face so beautiful—high cheekbones sharp enough to whet a knife on, brilliant deep-set black eyes—it defied even a hostile listener to look away while he spoke. Zara was her own defender, and the jury was Rachamim's motley gang of Arab and (several) Jewish youths. They met once a week to talk politics. Several camps had emerged, and there were all the signs that the trial would follow the usual lines for their arguments. Daud was spokesman for the group which proclaimed themselves, as Palestinians, the only rightful owners of the land, who said that the Jews had taken Palestine by conquest and the conquest was still going on. The Jews' nationalistic racist movement, Zionism, was completely invalid and any recognition of Israel, or willingness to compromise with it, was treachery.

Raif lead the opposing camp, to which Zara belonged, and which had Rachamim's tacit support. It was based on the premise that no people may declare another's national movement invalid. There had been two nationalist movements fighting for the same land: one had won, the other lost, but the loser's cause was not negated. Nationalism was only a path: the ultimate goal was an independent secular socialist society in all of Palestine. But Israel could not be changed while she oppressed the Palestinian people and denied their identity, for her own fierce nationalism stood in the way of true democratic socialism. The Palestinians must therefore return to the partition plan, agree to accept sovereignty over a part of Palestine only, and then reapproach Israel as an equal sovereign state. The working masses of both countries, freed from the distraction of nationalistic struggle, would then find common ground.

The trial began with a formal, restrained statement by Prosecutor Daud.

"Zara has expressed an intention to join the Zionist army next September. Since there are ways to get out of it, especially for girls, we must take it that she is willingly enlisting on the side of our enemy, the military arm of the Zionist oppressor. In the army, she will take orders. If they tell her to evacuate Arab villages to make way for immigrant Russian Jews, she will do it. If they tell her to shoot unarmed Arab demonstrators, she will do it. If they tell her to bomb refugee camps, she will do it or help other soldiers to do it, that's all the same. If they tell her to herd the free Bedouin into concentration camps because the land is wanted for Jewish kibbutzim and the Bedouin have no deeds to prove ownership, she will do it. If—"

"Stop!" Zara exploded. "I won't do it. I wouldn't do any of these things. I've not changed sides. Daud, you know me." But Daud didn't.

"Why are you going into the army?" Raif prompted her.

She was embarrassed. "I told you guys. I say you've got to defend the borders even while the real struggle goes on inside. I would refuse any orders against the Palestinians or the Bedouin."

"Then you admit you're willing to defend the Zionist entity!" Daud shot back, pounding the table once for emphasis.

"Okay, so I am. I never denied Israel; I just don't accept the tenet that its existence depends on the nonexistence of a Palestine. I know, Daud, you say that Israel is artificial, that it was created unnaturally by the Americans, the Nazis, the Russians, or whoever. The Israelis say the same about the Palestinian Liberation Movement. But it doesn't matter if Israel is a man-made invention. You know what that argument reminds me of? Frankenstein. Frankenstein made a monster, right, a man-made monstrosity, but somehow it happened that the thing came alive, it grew a soul, it became self-conscious. And when that happens, no matter what its origins or its heritage, it has a right to live."

Daud stared at her in cold affront. "That's a totally worthless emotional appeal."

Rachamim had a gentle way of speaking, that elicited goodwill from all sides. Raif said that when Rachamim spoke even the mosquitoes quit biting and strained to hear. He had taken such deep pleasure in the Raif-Zara romance that Raif had several times wondered if it was not vicarious; but the older man had never shown any sign of coveting Zara. Now he spoke quietly. "When I thought of bringing Arab and Jewish kids together, it was never with the idea that they would merge, that the Jews would become Palestinians or the Arabs, Zionists. I thought we could accept a degree of differing interests without being forced into opposing corners, while creating peace among us. It only comes through personal contact and friendship. We sit and drink coffee and talk, and Zara thinks, 'If that's an Arab, well then, okay,' and you think, 'If she's a Jew, there are possibilities.'

"It's never helpful to make impossible demands on one another. Don't ask Zara to deny her people to win your approval."

"It's the spread-your-legs-for-peace theory again," sneered the irreconcilable Daud. "Raif and Zara get it on together and you think you've solved the Middle East conflict. Personal contact, my friend, is not worth shit. Talking's not worth shit. Making peace means fighting on the same side, and action's the only expression of commitment. Zara's made her choice." He strode to the door, pausing to look back at Raif. "Now you make yours."

"What an exit," Rachamim said to the silence, but for once he was unfair. As Daud crossed the wadi alone, he wept. He loved Raif. When they were boys they'd fought shoulder to shoulder, and, for all his pride, Daud had been content to play lieutenant to Raif's captain. Daud was brave but Raif was fearless; he was leader because he could not be led. Occupation strengthened some Arabs and broke others, but somehow it had left Raif untouched. With never a show of unnecessary defiance, he went his own way; and before Zara crossed their path, Daud would have sworn that there was nothing under the sun that could sway him.

When Daud was suspended from school in ninth grade for tearing up his Israeli-revised history book, Raif had sat silently in the classroom. Daud felt betrayed, but the next

day, without a word to anyone, Raif disappeared. Four days
later he was back, with a sackful of history books and
Palestinian poetry. The books were Jordanian; how and
where he got them he told no one, not even Daud. For
weeks the boys met daily after school to study the precious
books. Then, one day, they came home to find the books
burning in a barrel in back of the house, while Raif's father
waited with a strap in his hand. He grabbed Raif by the hair
and cried:

"Do you know what the Israelis would do to us if they
found these books? They'd burn the house and put us out on
the street. Or into a refugee camp. You have no right to put
your mother and sisters into such danger." But the leather
dangled limply from his hand, and his tearing eyes could
not meet Raif's but kept straying to the burning books.

Gently, Raif untangled his father's hand from his hair
and walked to the barrel. The smoke was so thick he had to
turn his face away; but he stuck his arm inside and pulled
out a book. Tossing it at Daud's feet, he ordered him to
stamp out the flame, and again thrust his arm into the barrel.
His father reached him and pulled him hard to his body,
hugging him close to smother his flaming shirt.

But Raif had a man's strength now, and who was there to
pull him away from fiery Zara? His family could not move
him and neither could Daud, for all the leverage of his love.
Raif's choice was made.

There was a day when they sat in Rachamim's house,
listening to records. When Rachamim left the room, Raif
looked at Zara and said shyly, "You know, you're beautiful." He leaned away as he spoke; this was no advance, his
body said, but only friendly information. Zara blushed all
the same. "I am?"

He was the first; who else would tell her? Not Ruth. Not

Rachamim, or Micha, or any of her schoolmates. Zara's was a strange, embryonic, almost ominous beauty that boded ill: it was a mark on her and they would no sooner point it out than they would comment on a birth defect. But Raif saw her beauty without disturbance, and in speaking of it he changed it, gave it life, and was moved by it.

Another day, walking in the wadi, he took her hand and held it firmly until they emerged. Never once did he look at her, and when she glanced sidelong at his face she saw a confusing mixture of joy and grim determination. His hand, hard and dry, enveloped hers without diminishing it; his height made her feel taller. She imagined them as the incognito king and queen of the wadi, playing cou[...] sweethearts.

They planned a trip to Ein Gedi durin[...] decided to invite Rachamim and Daud. [...] sprained his ankle the week before, and so[...] forgot to mention the trip to Daud until too late, [...] went alone. They had to take three buses, one to Haifa, the next to Jerusalem, and the third to Ein Gedi. On the second bus he held her hand, discreetly. On the third he put an arm around her shoulders. As he did, the man behind them leaned forward and said angrily to Zara, "Is this Arab bothering you?"

"No!" she gasped; he sat back and hissed, "Disgusting."

Zara spun around and raised her voice. "Didn't you see us get on together? What business is it of yours, anyway? Just because—"

Raif touched her cheek. "Enough, Zara. What do we care what he thinks?"

"Nothing! He's nobody, anyway."

"So forget him."

She pretended to.

The winter rains had been generous, and the river ran full in Nachal Arugot. There were no other hikers, and despite the lateness of the day they saw groups of ibex come to drink. By the hidden waterfall, Raif pulled his hat over his eyes and said, "You creep."

Startled, she asked, "Why?"

"I think I love you."

About time, she thought, for she knew she loved him. Had known for ages, since his dusky body had begun to dazzle her, and his breath on her face caused an inner melting. But in her fantasy this scene had been more tactile. Did he think it showed respect, to bring up love with ~vered eyes and crossed arms, barricaded behind knap- start with? Didn't he want her?

said. "You don't love me on principle,

the hat and, raising himself onto one elbow, er. "What!"

I mean, to show that it doesn't matter about our religions and, you know, the Arab-Jew thing."

Raif laughed; it was another thing she loved about him, that unalloyed free-floating laugh of his. He assured her that his feeling was strictly apolitical and nonreligious.

Still he didn't touch her. She thought, the feeling might be apolitical, but the restraint isn't.

But when he did (weeks later, in their wadi), she suddenly grew shy. They had, at her instigation, swum naked for the first time, then lay side by side to let the moon dry them.

Raif turned to her, looked first at her face, then slowly at her breasts, the taut line of her stomach, the soft curve of her hip. He sighed, wanting her, yet feeling himself more sad than lustful. Zara held herself still, fighting down an

unexpected impulse to take refuge in her virginity and passively be seduced. Then she looked at him. He was beautiful. She held out her arms.

She'd thought she knew her body, but contrast gave it a deeper sense. When he touched her, she was filled with a sense of innocence and her first and only biblical awakening: they were Adam and Eve, before.

Beyond the wadi and over the hill, alone in a darkened room, Ruth knew. Her altered biochemistry instantly turned fear to anger, silent anger. She knew how to control her rage. Survivors know how to wait.

Now Ruth touched her hand and brought her back to the party. "Look who's here!" she said with unwonted gaiety, and thrust Micha toward her. He seemed embarrassed, but took her hand and asked her to dance.

She owed him secret thanks, she'd long ago decided, for helping her build up the strength to reject him and choose Raif. Soon the choice would be known to all, and she wanted him to feel her gratitude and share her happiness. They walked together onto the floor and he put his arms around her.

"You look beautiful tonight, Zara, more than any of the engaged girls, yet you're here alone. Are you so happy to be getting out, or do you have a secret lover?"

She smiled, letting him read what he could. "What about you and Tsipi?"

His face froze, his voice took on cadences of careful devotion, became a prayer of prior repentance. "She's lovely. We'll probably . . . Next year, when I finish the compulsory service . . ."

"Aha. What else will you do when you finish the army?"

"I may sign up for a few more years. Internal security

—it's important as hell and too few good people are willing to do it. Besides you make important contacts in the regular army."

She just looked up at him with the mocking smile she'd taken from him. Nothing he could say tonight would draw her into a political fight. She could indulge in silence, for he knew her well enough not to take it for acquiescence. Internal security, important contacts, indeed. Her lover waited down the hill, and she was as Arab as he was, dancing in disguise with the enemy.

A uniformed soldier wove among the dancers and ended up beside them, cutting in not on Micha but on her. He addressed Micha respectfully by rank and led him away. Her father came up smoothly before she could leave the floor and asked her to finish the dance with him.

Then the accordionist returned and swung the band into a driving hora. The party was at the stage of unaccustomed drunkenness in which it needed to move, and Zara was swept along. Henry held one hand, and from the sidelines her mother, uncharacteristically, appeared to grab the other. The dancers circled, three steps forward, one back, swinging arms and dipping with growing excitement. The spectators clapped in an increasing tempo and the speed invaded the bodies of the dancers. Someone broke the circle to lead them snaking into the crowd, weaving around the hall, doubling back to cross under the bridged arms of other dancers. Zara, electrified by the current flowing through interlocked hands, felt her private celebration merge finally with the group's. As she flung back her head, a slightly jarring image caught her diffused attention. Four or five men were walking down the hill, away from the conflagration of the dance. Through the dark she recognized Micha's walk. But her hands were pulled by her partner-parents, her

attention brought back to the dance, and fleeting apprehension was quieted by the thought that they were just going off for a quiet smoke.

But between mother and daughter there was still that telepathic link, that leakage of information. Ruth knew something Zara didn't, and when the dance ended and consciousness returned, Zara felt it. Turning to face her mother, she intercepted a look between her parents: it stank of righteous betrayal. A sudden image came to her, of those soldiers making their way down the hill while she jerked a marionette in her parents' grasp.

The menace of the image defied steady focus.

"Hope," Ruth said caressingly, but Hope didn't hear; instead, as if her fears had conjured it, she heard a shot, a cry. If what she feared was taking place, it was happening far out of earshot: but that quibble belonged to the grown-up laws of impossibility that slow Zara still had not absorbed.

She set out on a steady lope down the hill. The soldiers had a ten-minute start on her, but she knew the path blind.

Raif's little house was at the edge of the village, close to the wadi. Now, emerging from the wadi, she saw it in flames. Dark silhouettes milled around the fire, but she knew at a glance that Raif was not among them. Her pace never slackening, she ran straight for the door. Two meters from the house, with the fire hot on her face, she was tackled and brought down. With no idea who had tackled her, she fought viciously against the obstacle and felt some satisfaction at the grunts of pain she elicited. Then her attacker caught her hands and pinned her with unyielding strength, rolling on top to immobilize her legs. Micha, it was. On top of her again.

Blood, trickling from his mouth where she had gouged him, gave a red tinge to his words. "He's not in there."

She believed him. "Where is he?"

"Arrested. They took him away."

"What for?"

"Belonging to the PLO."

"That's a lie."

"He's guilty as hell. We found documents, evidence."

"Then he was set up. If it was you, Micha, I'll kill you."

There was no doubt that she would; but Micha's sudden fear was not of her threat but of the indecently clad pain she was allowing herself to show. Why the hell hadn't she f that way about him? They would never have been lyin the dirt like this if she had.

Zara sensed his vulnerability and hooked into it compellingly. "Say it, Micha. If you did it, say it."

For a lady pinned on her back, she commanded unreasonable strength. Unwilling even to answer, Micha heard himself saying, "No."

At Daud's house, there was no answer to her knock, but the door was unlocked. She walked in. The downstairs was deserted but something in the house was waiting. She went up to Daud's room and knocked again. After a long pause, his voice called, "Come in."

She opened the door. Daud sat on his bed, back to the wall, and a rifle in his arms pointed straight at her. His eyes were flecked with red and unfocused, but his hands held the gun steady. "Have you come to arrest me, Zara?"

A minor but noticeable incursion into her shell-shocked field. After a momentary jolt she ignored it, and the gun. "We've got to get help for Raif, get a lawyer out there to see him right away."

"Get one for me too while you're at it."

"If they haven't come for you already, they're not coming."

"Never mind, I won't need one anyway. They'll never take me. No fucking interrogation for me."

Now she knew what the red in his eyes was. Not fury or pain for Raif. He'd held a staring contest with fear, and lost. Who'd have thought it of fierce Daud? But she needed him, so her voice came at him softly, the way he'd always, secretly, wanted it to. "Come on, man. Raif needs his friends."

Daud laid the rifle down. "He needs you like he needs a rope around his neck. Because that's what you are, Zara."

Her face reddened with the impact of his words, even as she denied them. "No, the rope's around my neck too. The thing was aimed at both of us." Saying it she saw that it was true. Only the blow became doubly insidious, by appearing to strike only Raif. Daud's hatred was unyielding, and his eyes drove her back. But she was not so craven as to leave without asking her question. "Who set him up, Daud?"

"You should know."

But she didn't.

The need for allies, and her mother's teachings ("Loyalty resides in the family") rising in her like sap in an injured tree, drove her to Raif's family, no friends to her. A very young child opened the door to her and led her into a back room where the sound of weeping ceased as she entered. No men were present. Raif's mother and two sisters, attended by other women, sat on the floor. On her rare visits to this house Zara had been treated not with warmth but with punctilious courtesy. No one now offered her a seat or even a glass of water. She stood in the doorway on weakening

legs, regarding the face of Raif's mother, longing to join
their community of care for him, to weave a net of women's
love to support him, but her fibrous love was not accepted.
Raif's mother stared evilly at her, shriveling her exposed
heart. Blame was too light a word for the hatred in her eyes.
A hissing like escaping gas filled the room and nothing
could be said. Zara slunk out.

Arab children throw stones, and it's not the way Western
kids throw snowballs and spitballs, not a game at all. All
groups and stages have their functions in the strictly ordered
village society, and that of little boys is to stone strangers,
trailing them with cries of "Foreigner," to make their
comings and goings. Isolated Israeli settlements have their
armed civil patrols, their soldier guards; besieged Arab
villages have only impertinent raucous young boys armed
with stones and the questionable immunity of children. For
years Zara's presence in the village had rung no alarms.
How then was the verdict on her passed and promulgated so
quickly? Or was it spontaneously generated, the unanimity
with which they turned against her? As the gale of contempt
drove her from the home of Raif's family, jeering children,
tossing rocks and epithets of "Foreigner," drove her from
the village.

Exactly halfway between Tivon and Dar Ayun, Zara fell
onto the ground, paralyzed. Temporarily out of order,
unable to move, unable to cry, she brooded and attributed
blame. She'd thought that all her years of flaunted noncon-
formity had cost her nothing worth troubling over, nothing
but a loneliness which was good for the soul. But now the
true price stood revealed: the despicable ineffectuality.
Because they'd never sought others' acceptance of their
more-than-love, their kinship, now, with Raif her man in

jail, Zara had not even the right to sit with his mother and take a moment's comfort in shared grief.

If she had been his wife, no force could have kept her from his side now. If she had married him two years ago, the bond would have been inviolable. By leaving them separate and vulnerable, she had brought on this attack. Now the sweetest of her memories invoked the sharpest pain, but before going on, she needed to recall it.

It was a week after Daud's attack on her, a week in which they'd met daily, but Raif had said nothing more about her approaching induction. That night, in their usual place in the wadi, there was an urgency in his touch, a current of persuasion streaming into her which he tried to curb. He said offhandedly, "I've thought of a way to get you out of the army if you're interested."

She looked at him reproachfully. "I won't say I'm religious."

"Of course not, who'd believe you anyway?" and he kissed her. "Say you're married."

It was no joke, but she giggled in panic. "What do you mean?"

"Let's get married."

"But my dear child, Raif, you know that in this wicked state Jews and Arabs can't marry."

"They can in Cyprus. Daud's cousin has a boat that can take us, and he's willing. In a week you'll be eighteen, and you can get a passport without your parents' consent."

"Is it to save me from the army, fate worse than death, that you've come up with this?"

"No, fool, it's a sacrifice I want to make to save you from your mother." Raif could make jokes as cruel as her own, that twisted and plunged inside like swallowed knives. But, so close to her that she didn't know if it was said or just thought, she heard his reason: We belong with each other. In the face of so much opposition, there's need for affirmation.

And why, she thought now, bereft, sorrow erasing the face that Raif's touch had wrought, why had she said no? Vanity, that resisted her removal like stolen property straight from her parents' home to a husband's? Adventurism—join the army and see the world? And then come back to Raif, of course, that was understood, return to Raif who unfortunately has just been removed. One foolish choice and Zara had enlisted in the conspiracy against herself.

Enough self-indulgence; she picked herself up. While she sniveled with self-pity, Raif was being interrogated, probably beaten. His father and uncle would have gone to the police station, but she knew with what contempt the relatives of a suspected terrorist would be treated. Nothing mattered more than getting a lawyer to Raif. Having only one person left to help narrowed her choices, helped her move again.

She had to skirt the school to reach his house. The music was as loud as ever and through the windows dancers bobbed in and out of view; but outside the building, men stood in little knots. As she ran by, one dashed out to intercept her. It was Uri; with an oil slick for a voice, he said:

"Don't go too far, Zara. Haven't you heard?"

"What?"

"A bunch of terrorists were preparing to attack Tivon. They caught one, but there might be others." His avid eyes scavenged her face for reaction. She said nothing, but anger steamed through the look she gave him. Uri's face changed abruptly; he backed away and at a safer distance muttered, "Crazy bitch."

It didn't help. What could her frightening Uri, coward that he was, do to lessen the obscene horror of Raif branded a terrorist and torn from her? The disproportion congealed within her, making breathing difficult.

While she froze, Rachamim melted. When he opened the door to her pounding she was shocked by his face, like a ruined clown's, all lines streaming downward, weeping sweat. Like a man who's undergone torture but—she looked hard—hasn't broken. "Zara!" "Rachamim!" they clung and rocked and invoked hell for a few minutes.

When Daud phoned, Rachamim had listened to the news, thanked him politely, and hung up without asking a single question. Then he sat next to the phone for an unreckonable time, unable to react, replaying Daud's message in his head over and over. The next phone call, from Raif's father, broke his paralysis. He took all the information he could get, told Raif's father to take one witness with him to the jail and insist on seeing Raif. Then he called Ariella Stern.

Communist lawyer, Palestinian supporter, indefatigable defender of lost causes: Zara hadn't known Rachamim moved in such exalted leftist circles. Ariella had promised to leave Tel Aviv at once for the prison.

"Did you tell her why they picked on him?"

"I told her about you. She said it's better to keep you well out of it at this stage. Nobody likes uppity Arabs poaching on Jewish territory."

"But Raif was set up! How is she going to convince anybody of that if she doesn't tell about us?"

"She said it's better to attack their evidence. Since it's all fabricated, it won't hold up."

"I've got to see him."

"Zara, for God's sake, if you don't want to hang him, stay away."

"Stay away?" Hearing the rising note in her voice, he took tight hold of her. "I'm already half there. My stomach aches like it's been ripped out of my body and I can feel every goddamn thing they're doing to him. I can't stand it, Rachamim."

"Yes, you can. Because you know that they'll hurt him more if you go." He looked at his watch. "Ariella should be there by now. I was going to go over . . ."

"Why, do you think they'll let you see him?" she asked hopefully.

"No way," firmly. "I just didn't feel like sitting around waiting. But I won't go either."

She nodded. Never did learn to say thanks. "What are we going to do, Rachamim?"

"Care for a smoke and a game of backgammon?"


They played and smoked, smoked and played, until the music and the last passing voices faded out. Then they went on throwing the dice and making their moves in silence, leaning back against the cushions, till the dice and the numbers and the rising smoke became a barrier which nothing outside penetrated.

Then at last, Zara hung her head down and cried, silently at first, then giving way to deep sobs. No thought, but only fragmented repeated phrases ran through her head. "Do you have a secret lover?" "He's been arrested." "Guilty as hell." Rachamim kept away and she lost consciousness of him in the room; perhaps he left it. At last her tears stopped, her breathing softened, her mind grew quiet, with a kind of dying peace, and she let the cushions cradle her sinking body. Then it was she felt Rachamim's light weight dent the cushion beside her and felt him, through closed lids, studying her face. "Zara," his voice came soft and close and mellow, "don't you think you'd better go home?"

Eyes closed, she shook her head.

"Your parents will worry."

"They knew." She opened her eyes a little, looked at him through the slits. "I can't go home till that is explained. Will you let me stay?" He smiled and got up, disappearing into his bedroom. In a moment he was back, placing a sheet over her. Instead of calling it a good night he knelt and lightly kissed her forehead, and there was some comfort in it for her. Zara slept and dreamed.

In her dream she was on trial as a witch. The court was full of women from Tivon, all dressed up in long calico dresses and bonnets. The charges against her were vague, and the testimony ludicrous. One woman said that Zara had made the weather turn bad to ruin her vacation in France. Another claimed she'd seen Zara walk across a wet floor without leaving any tracks. In addition to this, the court was obviously biased. Zara asked the first woman who spoke whether she was witness, prosecutor, or judge. The woman replied, "It doesn't matter." Through all kinds of legal tricks, they prevented anyone from testifying on Zara's behalf, including Zara herself.

From the looks on the faces of the two judges, the verdict was bound to be guilty. And yet Zara couldn't believe it, because the only way they could have found her guilty was if they wanted to see her burn. Her mother, sitting at her side, urged her incessantly to escape before the verdict was pronounced. But Zara waited, incredulously, for the truth to come out.

It didn't, and she escaped just before they found her guilty.

# CHAPTER III

The days that followed had the same surrealistic air as her dream, and a tedium not passive but actively debilitating, punctuated by isolated moments of clarity. One of these occurred when Zara met Ariella.

She'd felt that immediate connection, that shock of clear seeing, only once before with a woman, and that was Carmen-of-the-park-bench, the invisibility player. She'd felt, with Raif, and Micha, and a few other boys, that embryonic surge which is neither love nor hate but the potential for both; but never again had it come with a woman, till the moment she clasped hands with Ariella. Ariella's beauty was concentrated in her malleable upper lip, capable of expressing whatever she felt but was constrained from saying aloud, and in the deep lines of her face, not one of which spoke of compromise or resignation. Ariella for her part saw beneath Zara's paradoxical beauty, her mad-dog eyes, to a core of self-possession startling in one so young. "You'll do," Ariella pronounced shortly, and Rachamim puffed, "I knew you two should meet."

After assurances that Raif was alive and relatively well, Ariella asked them about him. Zara had never had cause to describe him to a third person, and found doing so a painful act of near-introspection. She was more effective at describing his politics than his character; her adamant denials of any possible connection between Raif and terrorism were based on logic, not passion. She left it to Rachamim to describe Raif's gentleness, curiosity, his race-blindness and his love. Zara's was the more comradely, Rachamim's the more loving, mode of speech.

For an hour they talked, and Ariella listened. At the end she asked one question only: "Who hates him?"

Rachamim glanced delicately at Zara, who glared back at him, furious at the implication that she hoarded private information.

"He had no enemies that I know of," she said. "I am the one who makes enemies. Whenever we were hassled for being together, Raif was always for talking to the people and understanding them, while I would fly into a rage and want to break heads for an insult. Once when someone in a bar called me a whore and Raif my pimp, I hit the bastard with a bottle. But I stopped doing stuff like that when it became clear that Raif was the one who had to finish the fights I started. It was strange. People, all disposed to like me as a nice young Ashkenazi *maidele*, ended up hating my guts and calling me a fraud and an Arab in Jew's clothing: while people who don't like Arabs were always making unwelcome exceptions for Raif. You know, 'Such a nice boy, you'd hardly believe he was an Arab.' "

Ariella nodded. "Then why do you think anyone would set him up?"

"To put a wedge between the two of us."

"Who was most against the two of you as a couple?"

Trying to concentrate, Zara felt the first stabbing pains of a headache. "Everyone. Micha, the officer who arrested him, was an old boyfriend of mine. Uri Benzion and a bunch of the guys from Betar hated Raif's guts. Maybe even Daud was against us, but he'd never have chosen this way to break us up. And there are Raif's parents, but they'd have sent *me* to jail, not him." She stopped suddenly, lowered her head and rubbed it with her palm. Rachamim leaned over solicitously. "Do you have a headache?"

"A killer. I'm sorry. Rachamim, get me some aspirin please and we'll go on."

"That's enough for now," Ariella said, and signaled Rachamim to follow her out of the room.

"Wait, Ariella. When can I see him?"

Gently, "I'm sorry, you can't. No one but his lawyer is allowed in, not even his father. Would you like me to give him a message?"

"Yes. Tell him that I'm with him absolutely. Tell him that I'm buying us two tickets to Cyprus."

"I'll tell him. But, Zara, don't buy them yet."


At dusk Ariella and Zara went walking in the wadi. In pine-filtered light, Ariella looked grim, haggard, unconsciously beautiful. Trying to emulate her, Zara could produce only a zombie-like semblance of poise.

As they walked, Ariella explained. First: Raif was being held under the Emergency Regulations, enacted by the British in 1945 to control the Jews and retained by the Jews to control the Arabs. Under the regulations he could legally be held incommunicado, interrogated without a lawyer, incarcerated for months without a charge. In fact, he had already been charged, with membership in the PLO, participation in the planning of a terrorist attack on Tivon, and possession of weapons intended for use in terrorist actions. The trial had been set for ten days hence. If convicted of bad intentions, Raif could get seven years' imprisonment. Second: under the Emergency Regulations, the trial would be a military one. This meant that portions of the testimony pertaining to security or given by security men could be taken in a closed court. Third: There was no appealing a military verdict.

"Then it all depends on the judge he gets," Zara summed up.

"Quite," Ariella muttered, bending to examine a pinecone. Zara's heartbeat quickened, and she said. "You know who it is?"

"It's not good, baby. Judge Mordecai Reichman."

"I've heard of him. . . . Who is he?"

"Judges aren't supposed to have any politics. But Reichman once harbored political ambitions. He ran on a religious-nationalist platform."

Night came on as they walked. The air cooled and birds filled the sky. Soon the animals would emerge. The voices of the two women blended with the wakening sighs of the wadi. Zara asked, "And you say there's no appeal?"

"No appeal," Ariella answered sadly, feeling like a family doctor, with fatal news.

"I see. It all makes sense, except for one thing."

"What's that?"

"Why don't they save themselves the trouble and expense, and just take him out back and shoot him?"

In her prime Ruth had been an expert weaver and caster of nets that divided the world into us and them. The same sun that had transformed her daughter had shriveled and blinded her. Only Zara remembered Ruth as she had been, so only Zara mourned her diminishment, and pitied the bitter woman whom all the village disliked.

She'd been a terror, Ruth had, brilliant and intimidating. She'd had one friend in New York, a young art teacher in the school where Ruth taught history, and nothing in all of Hope's short life had pleased her as much as the sight of the two together: her mother, tall and stern, dressed always in solid dark colors, her regal posture turning the plain wooden chair into a throne, the linoleum kitchen into a court; and Jessie, the fair young American lady-in-waiting, bearing flowers and candies for the young princess Hope.

Hope used Jessie for a prism, to separate Ruth's dazzling beam into simple comprehensible rays. And Jessie shared Hope's mother worship. Ruth's gaunt beauty, her intense, guarded eyes and mysterious foreignness were intriguing enough; but Jessie came as an acolyte, not merely to admire but to learn, and Hope fed from the crumbs that dropped from their table. Even then she could make herself invisible, and rarely did either woman show awareness of her, save a certain warning snugness in Ruth's grip as she cradled her daughter's head against her tattooed arm.

With a book or a toy for camouflage, she would settle in Ruth's lap to listen as Ruth, with a newly developed gift of tongues, mimicked and mimed her way through the Holocaust. It seemed to her dazzled pair of listeners that there was nothing she couldn't do, no one she dared not impersonate. One day she was the impartial, scientifically detached professor of racism, lecturing to his class; the next, a sluggish victim-designate, with glasses too attuned to fine print to read the writing on the wall. She could act both the imperturbable civil servant, safe in the righteousness of

following orders, and the sheltered bourgeois Jew whose
wild outrage was fettered by his identical habit of obedi-
ence. Her imitation of the scramble-brained socialists,
scurrying for cover at the first sign of action's replacing
rhetoric, left Jessie laughing and tearful. And Ruth did not
spare the most pathetic of the bunch, comfortable man,
conservative by life-long habit, brought face to inhuman
face with his destroyers. Traumatically and belatedly radi-
calized, what a miserable failure of a revolutionary he
made. Then she said: "That man is my husband, Hope's
father. A good man," and "good" was lightly battered in
scorn.

Ruth felt a sensual delight, which was communicated to
Hope, in holding her own child on her lap while describing
the steamroller death enterprise that had somehow failed to
flatten her. There were times when Ruth's explanations
touched on shunted, stagnant pockets of emotion, and
Jessie would sit, schooled and unflinching, as these rose to
burst stinking upon the surface; but did the child understand? When Ruth began to speak about the camps, Jessie
objected.

"Surely this is not for Hope to hear, at her age?"

"Precisely at her age." Ruth turned the child around to
face her and stared into her eyes. "It doesn't matter whether
she remembers or forgets. I want it to be part of her."

Stunned at this direct communication, Hope resolved to
remember at least the words: missing bits of meaning could
come later. Jessie said, "You see everything through the
dark glass of the camps. It's only natural. But if you take
that into account, you surely cannot wish to give your own
vision to your daughter. Do you really want her to see the
world through the eyes of a survivor?"

"Whose vision should I give her if not mine? My eyes

have been purged, cauterized of all sentimentality. I know human evil and I *will* prepare my child for it."

"And who will prepare her for good?"

"I can't," Ruth said. "But no one dies for lack of that." Jessie did not answer but laid pitying eyes on Hope, who was oblivious, infected with Ruth's greatness.

"Listen. There's only one serious political activity for Jews, and that's making sure that next time the tanks begin to roll, we're behind them."

Poor Jessie, a good socialist, emanated distress. But did the wispy girl child seated at the table sipping milk understand? Of course not. Not immediately. How could she? But what need was there for understanding? She heard it all.

Now pity made her avoid her mother: she had performed no great broad stroke of avenging will, but a mere misdemeanor, a crime of silence. Clearly they had been warned to keep their daughter at the party and out of Dar Ayun at all costs, and they'd kept both the warning and its implications to themselves. Passivity was not quite treachery. In time she would forgive them. But now she had no energy to spare.

Everyone knew where Zara was. She sent Rachamim to tell her parents as kindly as possible to stay away.

She had other problems. She suffered a constant, throbbing, never-before-experienced sexual starvation, as though enforced separation from her mate had brought her into heat. She could have run wild through the village men with the cruel compulsion of her need, but for the impossibility of lying with the enemy. Nor would those timid men have had her, mad dog that she was. Some generous souls whispered that she should be put out of her flaunted misery.

A friend might have provided a solution, but who was there besides Ariella, a woman, and her beloved but somehow sexless Rachamim? It was clear to her: either Raif would go free, or she would die in an explosion of dammed-up sex.

There were fights with Ariella, yet beneath the acrimony lay a luxurious cushion of acceptance. It gradually became clear to Zara that not only was she barred from visiting Raif in prison, but Ariella wanted even to keep her out of court. She had envisioned herself mounting the witness stand, issuing a scathing denunciation of the charges, clearing Raif with her testimony, and quitting, on his liberated arm, a hushed and shamed courtroom. Ariella had a different scenario.

"Picture this, Zara. You're a witness for the defense, so I question you first. I ask you to tell the court what your relationship to the defendant is. What do you answer?"

Zara shrugged. "I'll say we're engaged."

Ariella snorted, "Reichman will love that. The man's a religious nationalist. In his eyes you're dirtier than dirt. You're wolves, tearing at the underbelly of his sacred cow. And he's God, Zara; he's the absolute and sole authority over Raif's fate. Besides, as Raif's fiancée you'll be presumed willing to perjure yourself for him."

"Then I'll say we're friends."

"Okay. I'm the prosecutor now, cross-examining." Her upper lip lifted sardonically, and her voice deepened and insinuated. " 'Just what kind of friends are you and Hawill?' I, naturally, object and get overruled. You say?"

"Good friends."

" 'Good friends,' " she mimicked in her prosecutor's voice. " 'You've just testified that your good friend Hawill is innocent as a newborn babe. You must know him well to give him such a glowing endorsement.' "

"I know him well."

" 'Intimately, would you say? How much time do you spend with your good friend? An hour a week? More? A weekend now and then? Every day, every chance you get? Where do you spend all this time together? Ah, in the wadi and in his room. Alone? And why don't you bring your good friend home with you? Why should your parents object to an innocent friendship with an Arab boy? What do you do alone in his room together besides discuss politics? Do you have sexual relations? Is he good?' "

Rachamim broke in, looking scandalized. "Ariella, for God's sake, they're not going to ask if he's good? That's your question."

Ariella grinned wolfishly and Rachamim blushed. But Zara glowered in deep, regal affront, like her mother contradicted. "Do you really think," she asked stiffly, "that I'm afraid of that, or ashamed to say that Raif is my lover?"

Ariella had a sudden vision of Zara standing with one foot over a precipice, enemy defiance exuding from every pore as she turned at bay to face her pursuers, unaware of the danger behind her. Desperate crises were the seas that Ariella swam in, staying mostly dry; what threatened were out-of-place emotional reactions like the one she was experiencing now, this compulsion to hold Zara back. Fortunate for her that Zara was too heavily armored to be broached, or Ariella might have ended up playing Joshua to her Jericho; and what might crawl out of those fallen walls was awful to imagine.

She answered in the flat tone of unmoved observation, the only tone with a chance of reaching Zara. "I don't think you're afraid of it. I think you're longing for the chance."

The pretrial nights took on a domestic pattern: light suppers of yoghurt and salad, followed by the ritual preparation of Rachamim's pipe and the setting up of the backgammon board. Zara played stolidly, registering numbers, combinations of numbers, calculation of odds, with a concentration so void of emotion that an hour of play rested her more than six of broken, nightmare-ridden sleep. Rachamim played as he'd learned, a boy in Egyptian cafés, elegantly and fast, without seeming calculation, the combinations so ingrained that a glance at the dice determined his moves.

Rachamim came from a deeply rooted line of Egyptian Jews: the cataclysm in his line had been not the Holocaust but the founding of the State of Israel, which uprooted the Jews of Egypt. His uncle had been lynched in the streets of Cairo on a spurious accusation of Zionist intrigue, his sister attacked and nearly raped. Rachamim led his widowed mother and sister out of Egypt, with no more of the extensive property than could be hurriedly liquidated and smuggled out bodily. He chose Israel not out of any ideological support or identification, but because it was now the only state in the Middle East that would have them, and he would not leave the region. But his mother hated Israel: the rude and squabbling people, the Spartan living, the foreign language, and most of all the condescension and disdain shown toward Jews from Arab lands. They called her primitive, she who had been raised delicately to speak French, with a smattering of Arab commands for the servants, to consider Paris her second home and the only place to shop, to be driven by chauffeurs, not jostled on overcrowded buses. After two months she had taken her daughter and fled to Paris, where she had friends and family.

Rachamim stayed. He built the house he lived in, and lived in it alone. He built a house with two rooms and two doors, one facing Tivon, the other overlooking the wadi and the village Dar Ayun beyond it. The front room he furnished in the style his Israeli neighbors favored, imitation Eastern Europe: Persian carpet, upholstered sofas and armchairs, glassed coffee tables and heavy curtains.

The other, the room in which he lived, was arranged on floor level, a simple rush mat covering the tiled floor, hassocks and low stools and two cushion-covered mattresses at right angles against the walls. Open windows behind bamboo shades let the breeze in and kept the sun out.

When they had been playing for an hour, a furtive knock came from the front room, on the Tivon side. It was close to midnight. Zara felt a sudden rush of hope: perhaps Raif had escaped and come for her. She was on her feet when Rachamim returned.

"It's Micha. He won't come in but he wants to talk to you."

Zara's face withdrew into the aloof, reckoning cast that was becoming habitual in their backgammon games: not an unhelpful attitude to carry over, Rachamim reflected, not an invalid one—but, she was losing two out of three games to him. Deep in calculation, Zara drifted out to Micha.

He was just outside the screen door, leaning against the doorjamb. She stayed inside but close enough for him to feel her breath on his face through the dividing screen. "Yes, Micha?"

His face was invisible but his words erupted like sparks

that he kept trying to smother with a damp blanket of a whisper.

"I thought you were crazy when you said Hawill was set up, but I asked around. When I found out who brought in all the information against him, and who initiated the raid, I got more suspicious."

"Who was it?"

"Never mind. I had a talk with him. Seems this guy figured I'd have some reason to approve of what he did. Anyway, he admitted it all freely."

"Admitted what?"

"That he'd received information against your friend, but no evidence. So he supplied the evidence."

She wondered about a trap, by Micha or through him, but couldn't see the teeth of it. "What did he supply?" Cautiously.

"The weapons, a map of Tivon with the schools marked, letters demanding an exchange of prisoners for hostages. He stole the weapons and forged the papers based on actual stuff he'd seen through the security forces."

"Who was it?"

"Forget it!"

"Tell me who it was."

He'd sworn to himself he wouldn't. But her voice forced him. She was not seductive but coercive, powerful in direct proportion to her burning desire to know.

"Uri," he whispered.

And while he still floundered in her current she drew in the net. She said, "Micha, you realize what you have to do."

He gasped. "But I don't know he's innocent. There was information against him."

"Who gave it?"

A long pause before he answered, "He wouldn't tell me that."

"Because it's a lie, like the rest of it," Zara exulted. "There's no such information because the whole thing's a fable, it never happened and never could. You can't go along with this thing. Not you, Micha, not even if you hated Raif."

"That's why I'm telling you. There's nothing else I can do."

"There's plenty more you can do. You can start by telling the court what you told me. They'll drop the charges."

"No way. It's just hearsay, inadmissible as evidence. Uri would deny it." He approximated a laugh. "You know the army bureaucracy. There's no way they're going to stop a trial that's already in motion till they get a verdict, preferably a guilty one."

"It figures," she said. "But even if we can't get the charges dropped, there must be a way of using this admission to force Uri to drop his testimony against Raif."

"I tried that."

"How?"

"I spoke to his commander. He told me to keep quiet and promised me an answer by tonight. And I guess I got it."

"What do you mean? What did you get?"

"My leave canceled and a transfer to another unit. Somewhere in the Sinai. Starting tomorrow you can reach me through the good offices of the army."

Halfway across the village he slowed to a halt, looked back at the house where she had found refuge. There was a churning in his stomach and an undefinable mood come upon him. There was a toothache kind of pain he could have named for her and perhaps did: "Zara," he heard himself mutter. "Sorry."

# CHAPTER IV

Like a dog laying a gnawed bone at its master's feet, she gave her information to Ariella, who was grateful but dubious. Zara asked why the lack of enthusiasm.

"Well, it is hearsay," Ariella admitted. "And we already were assuming that somewhere along the line Raif had been framed."

But when Raif came to trial, Ariella played the card for all it was worth in the devalued currency of the game, demanding a dismissal on the grounds of the main prosecution witness's long-standing hatred for the accused (this was rejected out of hand) and tearing into Uri when he gave his testimony. Since he was a member of the security force, the courtroom was cleared for his testimony; the only spectator allowed to remain was, strangely enough, a Dutch journalist. He showed Zara his notes during the recess.

Uri denied ever having known Raif until Ariella reminded him of the fight in the wadi, when Raif broke Uri's finger. Then:

"Why did you say you'd never met Raif before the night of the arrest?"

"I forgot."

"Did you like getting your finger broken, or did you resent it?" Ariella had asked. Uri replied blandly, "I didn't mind."

"How did the judge look then?" Zara demanded, and the journalist shrugged. "Bored."

When Uri had concluded his perjury, the spectators were allowed back into court. Witnesses for the defense were called—a parade of frightened, sincere friends and teachers who gave character testimony. A neighbor of Raif's swore that he'd seen an Israeli soldier sneaking out of Raif's house while he was out, a day before the arrest. Ariella rose to demand that the witness be allowed to view the security officer who had testified previously in a line-up, to see if he could identify him. The judge yawned his refusal: "You have been in enough military trials, Madam Stern, to know that identifying valuable security officers is the last thing we care to do." Daud did not appear, had not in the morning session either. Ariella said that he refused on the grounds that he did not recognize the court's authority to try Raif; but Zara suspected simple cowardice. Zara, uncalled, witnessed silently.

When it came to Ariella's summation, Zara listened but the words seemed to dissolve before they reached her. She felt immersed in a cushioning fluid, an element now inert and characterless but, with the right catalyst, potentially toxic. A single word would do it. Fragments of Ariella's speech floated languorously into her hearing: "the vengeful testimony of one man . . . exemplary record . . . politically minded, yes, what decent human being is not?—but never violent . . . framed . . . framed . . . framed."

Where was Raif in all this blabber? Where were the words that would pierce the sophistry and judicial fog to reveal the heart of the matter: Raif's innocence? Who could look into Raif's face and hear him called a terrorist? No one —therefore it followed that no one was looking at him. Raif turned his head slightly toward her, and the false courtroom light glistened off his high cheekbones, wings that gave flight to his face. He turned further, and across Lawyers' Gulf and Hangman's Gully their eyes bridged. His look carried with it an image, a deep memory of his smooth, brown naked skin pressed against hers.

The point was Raif's innocence, but Ariella was only allowed to argue his lack of guilt. Ceasing to speak in a hostile court meant admitting defeat, but she could not filibuster forever. When at last her words died out, Judge Reichman did not call a recess to consider, but spat his verdict out like a frog harbored overlong in his mouth: "Guilty!" he pronounced.

"Does the prisoner have anything to say before sentence is passed?"

Raif glanced at the two foreign journalists present in the court, and spoke in careful English, repeating each statement in Hebrew and Arabic.

"I'm innocent. False evidence was given against me, and all of it circumstantial, not one bit of evidence linking me to the weapons placed in my house. All our attempts to prove this have been blocked by the judge, who seemed at times to double as the prosecutor. If the defendant in this court had been Jewish, he would have gone free." Then he said, with a self-consciousness new to Zara, "Having been denied justice, I will deny you the satisfaction of hearing an Arab plead for mercy."

Throughout his speech, the judge had been whispering to

his clerk. The silence after Raif spoke recalled him, and he looked at Raif and said, "The court sentences the defendant Raif Hawill to seven years' imprisonment. Due to the violent nature of the crimes planned, and the defendant's refusal to cooperate with security officers, the court will also recommend that no parole be allowed."

Dead silence in the court. Two bailiffs converged on Raif, and security men gathered like maggots round the frozen body of Raif's family. Zara was left facing the judge with no impediment between them. As she walked toward him, her stiff-legged mad dog approach drew his eye. So feral was her look, so clearly threatening, the judge gave not a thought to the possibility that she was armed but instead put his hands to his throat. She would go for that, if she went. He squealed for a guard but Zara stood and delivered judgment. "Racist pig," she said, "I'll—" But before she could pronounce sentence her mouth was stopped by Ariella's hand.

Raif was being hustled toward a side door, when his captors' shock at Zara's blasphemy threw them off guard. Twisting sharply he freed himself of their grip and moved toward Zara, who had escaped from Ariella and was running to him. She threw herself against him; his cuffs dug into her back. The guards were converging. With only seconds for their parting, Zara whispered:

"I'll wait."

Already hands were prying them apart, but she leaned back into his bonds so that they could not succeed without manhandling her. It gave them another few seconds.

"Don't," he whispered, desperately. "You be free for both of us." He kissed her violently on the lips, broke off, and said, "I love you, Zara. Now get the hell out of Tivon!"

The courtroom was in pandemonium. Raif's mother

screamed: all the hate she'd held inside while the trial proceeded burst at the sight of her beloved lost son kissing the lips of his own despoiler. Reichman's reaction to being called a racist pig was as nothing to his shock at this damnable embrace, this nest of copulating snakes let loose in his courtroom. And Rachamim, the only still point in the room, had collapsed in his seat, disappeared into himself, his body an airtight, impermeable can of misery.

It took three men to prize them apart, and the marks of Raif's shackles stayed on her back for days. When they faded, she cursed the body which would not bear its proper scars.

Leaving the prison, Ariella and Rachamim walked on either side of Zara, but she refused their arms, declining to play the grief-stricken widow. Her man was not dead yet, and her primary emotion was not grief but rage. In the parking lot she saw Uri, leaning against a car, smoking a cigarette. As she moved toward him, Ariella and Rachamim, obedient seconds, fell back watchfully. Uri straightened up. Her own trembling ceased as she sensed his apprehension.

"Don't be afraid, Uri," Zara said. "I won't hurt you. Not with all these people around."

"I've got nothing to say to you."

"I can understand that; I'm not much of a talker either. I guess both of us prefer action to words." She took one step forward and he backed away unconsciously.

"You can't blame me. He was guilty."

"I know you planted that evidence. You've stolen seven years of our life; you've put Raif through hell. You've got to pay for that, Uri." Her voice was reasonable, almost friendly. "What do you reckon's a fair price for that, Uri?"

He always was in a way Zara's greatest supporter. Only

he believed in her image of her own power, which others considered illusory, if charming. Zara thought her look could, if not kill, then at least promise death. When she turned her evil eye on Uri, he panicked and tried to get away; but she had him hemmed in, pressed against the car behind him. He ended up bent over backward, spreadeagled against the side and roof. Till then she had not laid a hand on him. But seeing him ask for it, she brought her knee up, and slammed him viciously in the balls. Uri screamed: she recalled his screaming in the water, mothering a broken finger while she gasped half-drowned in Raif's virgin embrace. Now Uri was rolling on the ground. With an expectation of still greater satisfaction she pulled back a leg to kick him again. But suddenly Rachamim was upon her, hustling her away to the car.

"Zara!" Uri screamed after her, his face contorted with agony and humiliation. She turned. "You need someone to blame, Zara?"

"Uri, shut up!" Rachamim shouted furiously, but Zara, looked, turned back. "Blame your mother." Uri shouted. "She informed against him, she started this whole thing. You want revenge, Zara, that's the address."

In silence they drove back to Tivon. Ariella parked in front of Rachamim's house. Zara marched like a wound-up tin soldier in the direction of her parents' house. Her face was rigid, clear, emotionless.

Ariella called her name and laid a firm hand on her arm. Rachamim, too, struggled through the high gravity of his depression to reach her other side.

Perhaps with Raif gone she would have to get used to such violations of her freedom. But not without a struggle. "Let go," Zara ordered.

"What can you possibly say to her?" Ariella said urgently. "It may not even be true."

"It's true," bitterly. "It was criminal of me not to see it before. Everyone else did."

"I won't let you go." Never before had Rachamim hindered her, but Zara was beyond considering his changes. At that moment there was nothing to pity but much to fear in her. Her eyes measured them contemptuously. Friendship was forgotten; they were nothing but obstacles now.

Before she could strike, Rachamim said quickly: "You're not equipped for this yet. You know only one way to confront an obstacle and that's head on, with maximum force. You'd smash yourself up on this one."

Ariella whispered in the other ear: "Listen. It's true that there are some painful things that have to be done. You're wrong to think that the degree of pain involved is any measure of the thing's necessity. What I mean is, it's all right to let friends do some of the pulling for you. I'll talk to your mother. You take it all as said. Wait at Rachamim's. I'm going to take you away."

It was not their urging that defused her, not the balm of their concern which barely penetrated the surface of her anger. Rather it was the enforced pause which let her think. She could not face even in imagination the realization of her present desire. Clear it was that Ruth deserved to die, and clear that Zara could not do it. But any response less than murder would be a disparagement of Ruth's crime.

I'll come back, she promised herself, when I'm stronger.

Ariella left the car and walked toward Ruth's house. It was on the other side of town, a fifteen-minute walk, and she was hatless under the burning afternoon sun; but she needed time alone. What had it meant, that unplanned, "I'm taking you away"? Was she at this late date embarking on a new profession, social worker to the victims of her unsuccessful defenses? What the hell would she do with Zara if she did take her away? And how would she keep her out of harm, short of imprisoning her in a cage? She had no desire to return to Tivon to defend a case of matricide.

The village smelled of scorched earth, every footstep stirring up clouds of dust hot as ashes. She felt stifled. August was a month to drive people mad. They tried so hard, the villagers, planting trees and shrubs and pathetic lawns; and every August the parched, dust-encaked land and dying trees reproached them for watering false hopes. August was kinder in the south, where the desert permitted no wintertime illusions of green grandeur.

Thinking this, the answer came to her. Let Zara go down to the desert. The girl had an unfortunate allergy to anything resembling a home or a community. The desert was a well-known cure for allergies, and no community, only the stray individual, could set down roots in its barren soil. Let her go to Ronar. She was strong enough.

Ruth's house was shuttered and closed in on itself, like every other house in the burning August afternoon. Not a child or a dog or even a chicken could be heard or seen moving. Just a crazy communist lawyer. She walked up to the door and knocked.

Watching through a shutter the woman's slow, deliberate approach, Ruth guessed who she must be. She threw open the door and demanded, "Where's Hope?"

Interesting to see a woman whom so many people hated. Ariella had expected a stark embodiment of the antilife force, a gnarled inverted energy sucker, a black hole of a woman. But Ruth in the flesh was a vital presence, tall and straight, looking no older than Ariella. In fact it was like looking at a kind of mirror inversion of herself, a physical resemblance in height, coloring, and the strong lines of character, which in Ruth had grown differently in the expression of a different role. The eyes, of course, were wrong, black holes indeed, which absorbed but did not radiate: this she had expected.

Ariella said, "Your daughter has just had some shocking news. May I come in for a moment?"

As Ruth stepped back to let her in, Ariella glimpsed in the background a stooped gray man who scuttled out of the room.

"What news?" Ruth continued when they were seated, Ariella on a sofa, Ruth on the edge of a hard chair. "That Arab was convicted?"

"That was a foregone conclusion, once the accusation was made, and I think Zara had almost come to expect it before the trial. It's worse. She was told who made the original accusation." Ruth's reaction was neither denial nor any attempt at self-justification. Instead she asked calmly, "Who told her?"

"Uri Benzion."

While Ruth's thoughts dwelt on Uri, Ariella studied Ruth. The resemblance was there, she thought, but whereas Zara only imagined that her look could kill, the mother's probably could. Then, "I did not survive the Holocaust," Ruth said haughtily, "to see my daughter marry an Arab."

Guessing that she, like Zara, would only hear what shocked her, Ariella said with a show of anger, "Don't you dare use the Holocaust as an excuse. You've nearly ruined your daughter's life with that ploy already."

"What the hell do you know about it?" Ruth screamed. "You arrogant bitch, what do you know about it?"

"Enough."

"How dare you judge me! I've gone through more than you in your worst nightmares could conceive of. I've been—"

'Purged," Ariella mocked, her incorrigible upper lip curling, "reforged in the fires of hell, to arrive at a crystalline vision of the truth."

No one could question her camp-forged sanctity, inadequate compensation that it was. Ruth felt a wave of fury pass through her so intense and uncontrollable that in a moment it seemed she must either murder or convulse.

It was then that Ariella grasped the sleeve of her own blouse, jammed it up to her shoulder, and said, "My membership card."

Ruth stared at the exposed tattoo in utter disbelief.

"Shall we trade stories?"

Ruth's hands trembled as she lit another cigarette, but her voice remained level. "I have always feared that it was my daughter's destiny to relive my experiences. That is why we brought her here, and why, when I saw her threatened by that Arab, I took action."

"Threatened?"

"He was going to marry her."

"Did that threaten her, or you?"

"It's the same," Ruth snapped, then corrected herself: "Married to him she would never be safe."

This far and no further, thought Ariella; I don't want to hear any more. Ruth said, "I didn't survive Auschwitz in order to lose my daughter to the Arabs."

"And to prevent that, you were willing to sacrifice not only an innocent boy and his family, but also your daughter's happiness."

"Sacrifice? The only sacrifice here is my own, my happiness for my daughter's safety. I know she'll hate me

for a while. But my daughter of all people must learn that
survival requires hard sacrifices, that survival entails loss.
How else will she be able to resist her enemies?"

"What enemies?"

"You fool," said Ruth with loathing.

"I mean," Ariella drawled, "where is she ever going to
find an enemy as hard on her as you are?"

Ruth reeled but retaliated. "I told my daughter everything, but I didn't tell her about people like you. Your type
isn't new. Even during the war there were Jews who
collaborated with the Nazis. I tried to hide that one tiny
piece of filth from her, and this is the result. She falls into
the very hole I covered up."

Ariella, very white, said brittlely, "I didn't come here to
argue with you. But some things cannot go unanswered. Far
from collaborating, I ran away from home to join the Jewish
Czech partisans. I fought, and I killed. I was captured late
in the war and slated for death. I make no claims to
superiority on that ground, but I will not be called a
collaborator by the likes of you."

"Whatever you did in the war, you're now fighting
against your own people."

"Racists are not my people."

"I will not listen to this! Get out of my house."

At the door, Ariella spoke with restrained but strong
emotion, holding the other woman's eyes. "Ruth, I understand you. You would do anything to protect your daughter
from all that we experienced. Can't you see that you
yourself are re-creating that hell for her, forcing her to
relive it? Don't you see the role you've cast yourself in?
You informed falsely on that boy. Didn't the action mean
anything to you, remind you of anything? Ruth, you are a
sleepwalker; wake up!"

Every bit of survivor skill she possessed went into keeping Ruth's face blank, her voice impassive. "Send my daughter to me."

Ariella, defeated, said sadly, "Better not. She's leaving with me."

"She'll be back," Ruth crowed, displaying her triumph at last. "Hating or loving, we're bound for life. She'll be back."

In his house Rachamim had collapsed on a bed, depression fathoms deep in his open staring eyes. When Zara touched him, he quivered all over. The pain had surfaced and spread. There was no one to say good-bye to.

Zara threw her belongings, hastily jammed into plastic bags, into the back of Ariella's car and got in beside her. Driving through the village, they were watched, but not hailed. Zara stared impassively forward. As they circled the village toward the main road, there was a flash of movement from the side of the road, and suddenly Ruth, showing a face of naked desperation, tore through a hedge and ran in front of the car. Ariella had to jam on her brakes. As the car slowed, Ruth threw open the passenger door and grabbed Zara's wrist, pulling her out with a cry like a wounded bird of. "Hope! Hope! Hope!"

Zara allowed herself to be dragged from the car, then faced her mother. Of its own volition, her arm drew back, paused, then traced a wide slow, powerful arc through the air that ended with stunning impact against Ruth's cheek.

As they drove out of town, Ruth's screams of bereavement trailed after them. Zara switched on the radio.

# PART II

## THE DESERT

# CHAPTER I

Take a hawk's-eye view: white salt mountains, barren remains of ice-age buckling, swept-away landscape. In the distance, beyond the hills, down the great canyon, the sea gleams through pulsating waves of heat. Spiraling water erupts from the mountain's throat, through the mouth of the canyon. Twittering starlings and bulbuls weave patterns in the air in front of the waterfall, but scatter as the hawk shadow touches them. Along the inner walls of the canyon, white vertical lines crisscross the rock, paths of the ibex; below, deeper, wider grooves mark the paths of men. Sun at apogee: nothing stirs. From the mouth of the canyon, the water winds and tumbles down white rock, one great waterfall, then a descending series of smaller falls and linked pools. A flyer has his choice of pools to drink from; a climber risks life and limb for each gradation.

Besides a middle pool, alone, a motionless figure sits in the shade of an overhanging ledge. Only a hawk's vision could spot it, and only by the subtle expansion-contraction of its breath.

Leave the canyon, descend to the sea and swing to the left: far to the north, where the Jordan empties into the Dead Sea, there are fish.

Leave the hawk, return to the canyon in the body of an ibex, more skilled in vertical than in horizontal runs. Evening, and under a darkening sky the wilderness awakens. Scaling the walls of the canyon where now all manner of crawling, gliding, digging, hopping, running, slithering creatures have appeared, the ibex spots a human figure reclining in the water. Its utter stillness poses no threat.

It is Zara.

Climbing lightly onto the ledge, she turns her back to the water, stretches, and converts the stretch into a backward dive. Her body pierces the water like a piece of ribbon and emerges facing her point of entry.

Her eyes are as serene, deep, and thoughtless as the mountain pool.

Ariella dumped her there. They spent only one night in the apartment in Jerusalem, fighting all the time. Zara had trailed the lawyer through her large apartment, needling, accusing her of mishandling, even sabotaging Raif's defense. Ariella was sensitive, wondering if a desire to spare Zara had weakened the defense's claim of a frame-up. Finally, backed into a corner with Zara's curses flying at her, she reached out and slapped the girl. Zara answered with her fists, and a short brawl ensued. At the end of it, Zara, to her own astonishment, found herself pinned to the floor with Ariella's knee in the small of her back. As soon as she ceased struggling, Ariella got up and walked away. The next morning, she announced that she was going to Eilat for a few days and would drop Zara off in Ein Gedi.

raised her buttocks, and watched her face as he entered. Her climax came, and stayed. Only when he sensed her exhaustion did he allow himself to finish, and then he turned his face away. She didn't care. She was lost.

Much later she lay in bed by his side, smoking, beginning to think, while he lay stiff, silent, and watchful. There was no way she could stay in Ein Gedi and forgo sex with this man. Ein Gedi was refuge—she needed to stay. Sex meant absorption and there was no doubt who, here, was the stronger. It was so clear to her that she forgot all her Ronar lore and, meaning to surrender graciously, asked, "Shall I move in here?"

By his stillness she knew she had said something very wrong. She felt such a shame as she had not known since her concentration camp faux pas in kindergarten.

"No," he said after a moment.

"How come?"

"I live alone. Not only that, I sleep alone." Though his voice was gentle, she had the words interpreted before they reached her ears. Shuddering, she jumped out of bed, dressed quickly, and left. He never stirred.

When he came to her room the next night, she let him in, and let him in: a stunning surrender. But she knew, with the sense she never questioned, that there was in this coming of the mountain to Mohammed an intended expiation.

There was no question of betraying Raif. The best part of her was imprisoned with him. Ronar was her parole, earned by good behavior, but true pardon would come only with Raif's release. He'd sent her body away, with instructions to live in some other place and, obediently, she lived. She adapted to the desert, adapted to the solitude, adapted to Ronar. Every night before retiring to her cabin she looked at

the stars, imagined herself drawn up into the dipper and
rocked there with Raif. Ariella had told her not to try to see
him, not even to write. Zara protested: what further harm
could they do him? But the lawyer insisted. "He has to live
in prison, not you. If they learn about you, and there are no
secrets in jail, the Jews will attack him, and the Arabs will
turn away. Don't write."

She wrote, though, long letters about the desert, the
loneliness, the people of Ein Gedi, and the future. Their
future together, in some other country where Arab and Jew
could live together. Not even Ein Gedi could tolerate that.
No shame, but pity for his enforced celibacy, kept her from
telling him about her relationship with Ronar.

She sent the letters to Rachamim, to smuggle in as safely
as he could.

Raif was the framework of her life, Ronar possible only
within that framework. How else could she tolerate his
coldness?

# CHAPTER II

There was nothing unusual about the chartered Egged bus pulling into the Mayan David parking lot, except the passengers. Not the usual foreign tourists or Israeli nature freaks: these were orthodox Yeshiva girls, fifteen, sixteen, seventeen years old, spilling from the bus, chattering in Yiddish-accented Hebrew.

Zara was drinking a Coke and lolling in the shade with Beni, the field school driver. Unnoticed by the girls, they stared as half a dozen bewigged matrons, several no older than Zara, headed toward the kiosk. One cried stridently: "Only the bottled juices, girls! No ice cream—it's not kosher." They stank of innocence. Beni nudged her.

"Go over there."

She thought his interest in observing the contrast was prurient but didn't mind: she had a fancy of her own to satisfy. She wanted to come upon them like an apparition and spook them into scattered flight, the way she and Raif used to do in Jerusalem. It had been a favorite game. One of them would cut school (one had always to cut, since her day off was Saturday, and his was Sunday). They'd hitch or take a bus to the gates of the old city in Jerusalem, then stroll through, hand in hand, heading for the Western Wall. Invariably, somewhere along the way they would come upon a flock of Hasidic men. Then, as Raif fell back, Zara raced forward, heading for the heart of the cluster. Seeing her, the men averted their eyes; at the last moment, to avoid contact, they were forced to scatter, like seagulls taking flight before a runner on the beach. Sometimes she sang or laughed, and then the strictest among the Hasidim, who believed that a woman's voice in laughter or song was a clarion call to damnation, covered their ears.

As the girls noticed her approaching, their chatter died and they stared. She was female, as they were, but could have been of another species for all the outward resemblance there was. The orthodox girls were clothed from head to toe, and their virginal faces, neatly coifed beneath kerchiefs, shone transparently. Zara was naked but for shorts, sandals, and a bikini top: her skin was burnished deep bronze and her unkempt self-cut hair glowed gold. She wore a sheathed knife on her leather belt. The girls didn't move. Zara frowned and said, "Boo!", weakly. They smiled. She understood that there was no challenge to them in what she was: she was too different, a human animal to them, a feature of the Nature Reserve.

Beni disagreed, as he told her when she retreated in confusion.

"They recognized a kindred soul."

"Are you crazy?"

"It's true. Your nakedness has become as devotional as their modesty."

"You've got me wrong. It's purely functional."

Later she looked at her face in Ronar's shaving mirror. True that her face had acquired a kind of cloistered silence and that she looked far younger than she was.

The rebellious attitude of her face disturbed Zara. It wasn't right. If her mother had walked out of Auschwitz looking like Zara did now, she would surely have scarred herself, not to give the lie to the Holocaust. It was intolerable that Zara's face should not bear witness to what she herself had witnessed. Only her eyes refuted that illusion of peace.

But living on a remote Nature Reserve, however far her thoughts ranged, she was still among the protected species, sheltered by the ragtag camaraderie of the Nature Reserve's crew of misfits. Waves of political disruption bounced off the walls of this place, conflict excluded by its nature, which was harmony. They had no television. There was a radio at the field school but neither she nor Ronar had one. Newspapers came sporadically, days late; mail was rare; visitors few. Only occasionally was there an issue to disturb their tranquillity, and then it was usually Beni, their link to the outer world, who brought it.

He appeared at dinner one night after a week's absence and announced, as one item of gossip among many, that the Reserve Authority was thinking of expanding the boundaries of the Ein Gedi Reserve.

"Where to?" Eli asked.

"To include all the land up to the kibbutz boundary, and south as far as Wadi Darage."

"But that's Bedouin land," Zara said. "Can the Reserve Authority just do that?"

The men exchanged glances. Ronar said shortly, *"They* can't. It's government land and government doing."

"Why do they want to extend the Reserve?"

Beni was glib. "The Bedouin's black goats are destroying all the vegetation in the wadis. Everywhere they go, they create more desert."

"But the Bedouin have always lived here, and they've always kept goats."

"Yes," Beni answered, "but they haven't always had trucks. The occasional drought used to keep the numbers of the herds down naturally. But now, if there's a drought in the south, the Bedouin truck their goats up north, so there's no control over the size of their herds. There's already a problem keeping them out of Nachal David."

"Not as long as I've been here," she said slowly. That had been over a year.

Beni looked annoyed. Ronar said indifferently, "It's nothing to do with the goats," and the subject was firmly dropped. Later, in the jeep, he told her curtly, "They want to move the Bedouin into reservations near Be'er Sheva. It's political."

"What will you do?"

His face was cold. "It's nothing to me. If it means extending the borders of the Reserve, I'll help with the evictions."

And not for love of the flowers and the birds, she thought, but to expand his private domain. He was lord of Ein Gedi. It was not really a critical thought; she too had come to believe in the principle of exclusion.

She wanted, like Ronar, a wider prison: a legitimate goal for a prisoner. But she kept imagining Daud's scornful face. In her imagination she defended herself, telling him, "It's not appropriating land from Arabs to give it to Jews. No one will use this land. It'll be protected." She could see Daud's sharp eyes rejecting this. He would say, "Why don't you 'protect' kibbutz land then? Why Bedouin land?" And

Rachamim would turn to her, kindly but expectantly, and she would have no answer.

But she sheltered in the knowledge that the Reserve's function was nonpolitical and protective, and Ronar, too, was apolitical: he disliked all intruders equally and would just as happily evacuate the kibbutz as the Bedouin camp. More happily, perhaps, because he had more conflicts with the kibbutzniks than with the Bedouin. He also had a friend among the Bedouin, which he had not among the kibbutzniks, the clan's fiftyish headman, Mustapha.

Zara met him in the third week of her life in Ein Gedi, a few days after she started lying with Ronar. Mustapha was in Ronar's room when she reported after work. Ronar introduced them.

Dark eyes rested on her for a moment, then on Ronar, and Zara knew that he knew. But his dignified, wrinkled face showed no sign and he addressed her in courtly, resonant Hebrew: "You are welcome to Ein Gedi. My daughter told me of your arrival."

"I didn't meet your daughter."

"She saw you. But she is shy."

"Please tell her that I hope to meet her soon." Ronar looked at her with more than his usual impassivity, and she realized she'd unconsciously switched to Arabic. It had pleased Mustapha, but still she wondered why she'd done it. Ronar was far less her lover than her boss, and she'd just handed him a loaded weapon. There was nothing wrong with speaking Arabic, but she was sure that exposure of her past would end her life in Ein Gedi. Had she meant to signal Mustapha, declare herself an ally? As if he needed her! Perhaps she'd simply donned Raif's language as she would have his shirt, for comfort. But Ronar never mentioned it, so it didn't matter.

Months went by and nothing more was said or done about the land confiscation. It was easy to bury inconclusive doubts. The climate was not made for anxiety: it absorbed excess energy, leaving its humans high and dry. The wind that blew morning and night from the wilderness eroded the jagged corners of her thoughts till her doubts were as submerged in her as she was in the desert. Peace and calmness were shellacked imperfectly on to her face, but the signs of hidden passions gave her an erotic force of which she was entirely unaware.

Before she had been in the area six months every man had tried his luck with her. But this told her nothing about herself; she assumed merely that she was learning the ways of the world and attributed their horniness to proximity and her coming of age, never to the attraction of buried turbulence.

They came bearing gifts, flattery, and promises; dim Yossi even tried rape. He caught up to her on a moonlit walk along the shore, mumbled a few words, then shoved her to the ground. She kicked up vigorously and happened to catch his nose with her foot. Blood spurted, Yossi grew faint, and she had to help him home.

Beni was the only one to get close to Zara. His tactic was attack, not physical but psychological.

He was a wiry, hyperactive little man, ugly and smart, with a self-confidence as wide as the desert. On his days off, he often found out where Zara was working and hiked out to meet her. One day, a week after the Yeshiva girls incident, he followed her into Nachal Arugot. After an hour's hike through the deserted wadi, he came to the small trail leading into the Canyon of the Hidden Waterfall. Years of part-time living on the Reserve had taught him to move silently even through water. As he rounded the final bend in the stream, he saw her.

She lay on her back, toes in the water, face covered by her straw hat. She'd removed her bikini top and was sunbathing naked but for a pair of brief denim shorts. In one hand she held an orange, which she peeled blindly with the other. Her body was the color of dusk in the wilderness, punctuated by two rosy nipples and the white strips of her sandal straps.

Beni looked hard for a long moment, then moved forward, splashing as he went. Zara looked up, reached for her top.

"Well, if it isn't the Ein Gedi nun. Sorry to interrupt you at your devotions." He hunkered down beside her. "My, what a lovely body you've got." He sighed. "I could do fabulous things to it."

She laughed at him, not at all threatened, and fastened her top. Beni flushed. "What a waste."

"I don't feel wasted."

"I don't feel wasted," he mimicked. "A woman like you marooned in an oasis in the middle of a desert in a country most people don't even know the name of. You're so wasted you don't even know you're wasted."

"Do you want to take me to the Casbah, Beni?" she mocked. "Dress me in satin and pearls and display me in casinos and hotel lobbies?"

"I know you're out of my class," he said stiffly. "I just happen to think you're out of Ronar's as well."

She sat up and dared him with cold eyes to say more.

"Did you really think it's a secret? I've been up to see you more times than you know. If you're not in your cabin then where else could you be? One time I went over to Ronar's and looked in the window. I saw you sitting in a chair, with him standing behind you, and his hands running all over you. I saw that!" He ached just remembering; it had made him mad.

"Ronar would love that," she threatened.

"Then tell him! I'm not afraid of him."

Liar, she thought, but said, "I'm going back to work."

Beni grabbed her wrist. His eyes seemed unnaturally clear. He said, "I'm telling you, Zara, to get out of this place. You're dying here and you don't even feel it. You do nothing here but work, sleep, eat, and fuck a man who won't even talk to you. It's an animal's life."

A nerve beat in Zara's head. He had come far too close to her private image. She secretly saw Ronar and herself as two fine desert animals, fucking.

"It's a good enough life," she said. "Besides," she added, thinking of Raif, "I have good reason to be here."

Beni's eyes were scornful. "What reason! You think that ice-cold fucker loves you? He cares about no one! Did he tell you he's got a wife?"

Her cheeks declared that he hadn't, but she said stoically, "I never asked."

"He deserted her. Every once in a while the police come down to try to shake some money out of him, and your hero hightails it into the hills to wait till they've gone. That's your lover."

"He's not my lover," Zara said, and shook off his hand. As she stalked off, he called after her softly. She stopped, but kept her back to him.

"When you're ready to leave, tell me and I'll go with you. I've got money saved and I'll take you wherever you want to go. But if you won't have me, just choose your man. There's not one of us you couldn't rely on. Except Ronar."

Beni told the truth, Ronar was married. At twenty, he'd married a girl from a neighboring kibbutz, which had awarded them half a house, standard lodgings for new couples. Proximity stifled communication: after six months of the coupled life, he had nothing left to say to her, and her desperate, empty conversation grated on his nerves. When resentment sharpened to hatred, he left her, drifted down south, lived in the wilderness by hunting until he took a job with the Nature Reserve Authority. He offered her a divorce, but her bitterness and humiliation required appeasement, and she demanded his monthly salary as alimony. Ronar stayed married.

Later, she met a man and wanted her freedom. Then she wrote to Ronar, asking for a divorce without alimony. It was his turn to refuse. No law could compel him, and his marital status was a welcome impediment to any future emotional adventure, in the unlikely event that he should ever feel tempted.

In fact he had not been. Ariella was the only woman he really liked. Though they made love, on rare occasions of propinquity, with tenderness and enthusiasm, there was never a question of her sharing his life, or he hers, nor was there room for compromise. She had a political mind, a city body. He was a desert man, a hunter who excelled in trapping, who refrained from killing his quarry not out of sentimental nature-love, but because it was the condition of his employment. Instead, he tagged the animals he caught and set them free.

His sexual needs were met by the steady flow of women tourists through the Reserve, many of whom were attracted to him. It was convenient and neat except for the occasional messiness of tears, caused by his refusal to actually sleep beside any of the women he seduced.

That was fastidiousness, and habit. He'd thrown Zara out of his bed for another reason, one he could barely admit to himself and never would to her. The reason he refused to sleep beside her was that he wanted to.

Too much of one woman was unhealthy. Even accidental fidelity gave rise to bad dreams and troubled sleep. When he woke in the mornings thinking of Zara, Ronar cursed Ariella. What good did it do to kick the girl out of his bed when she had infiltrated his dreams?

He considered getting rid of her, but it was difficult. He liked women's bodies, even though he despised their inhabitants. Yet Zara seemed to lack those feminine traits he detested. She never clung, giggled, wept, flirted, or fawned. But deep inside her there had to be some feminine flaw. Had to be.

While working on her seduction he'd had no other women. That abstinence, justifiable then by tactical considerations, was no longer wise.

Within a few days his decision was rewarded with a busload of young Swedish girls. It was easy: Ein Gedi's subversive, tantalizing beauty ripened them so that all he had to do was choose and pluck. He chose and brought her to his room.

At six o'clock Zara came down from Mayan David, showered, and put on fresh clothes. At seven she was waiting by Ronar's jeep, but he didn't come. Thinking he might have fallen asleep, she went to his cabin. "Ronar?" she called to no response. She pushed open the unlocked door and walked inside.

And walked out, face burning. Now, she thought, I'll have to walk all the way up to the field school, and I'll probably still miss dinner. Bloody, inconsiderate bastard.

In his room Ronar was still seeing Zara's eyes, in their color perfect reflections of his, through the vacuous eyes of the stranger in his bed. He'd caught their momentary paling; he'd seen in them a reeling that her face and body concealed. It gave him information that Zara, at once too ignorant and too controlled, would never willingly have surrendered.

The moment Zara entered the room, the familiarity of her face had been in sharp relief to the impermeable strangeness of the Swedish girl's. That close familiarity was painful, but it was a pain to be relished. Knowing Zara was like chasing a swift deer up a mountain; and when hunting he'd never begrudged the pain, nor blamed it on the mountain or the deer.

"Darling, who was she? Who was that woman?" Darling, darling—he looked coldly at the girl—she only called him that because she couldn't pronounce his name. She'd been a disappointment anyway, because he couldn't help comparing her sweetness to Zara's tartness, her flaccidity to Zara's tautness. She'd had nothing to surrender. "Go now," he told her, "please."

He'd planned it; he'd timed it so that Zara would discover them. But he'd neglected to plan his own reaction, and hurt himself. He knew Zara, but he didn't think it the business of a man to know himself.

As she walked to the field school, Zara's eyes burned and her stomach ached. She thought, lucky I never depended on him. Lucky I don't need him. And she worked at suppressing her feelings, for her appearance at dinner.

The meal was almost over when she arrived, but there was food left in the kitchen. She helped herself and sat between Beni and Eli.

"Where's Ronar?" Eli asked, too innocently.

"Busy," she said. "Pass the bread please."

He laughed. "Up to his old tricks, is he? I saw him driving a blond tourist up to his place. That guy!"

She felt Beni's tension but refused to meet his glance. She went on eating stolidly until she came to the coffee. The coffee was too much. The coffee was so incredibly bad that suddenly she felt close to tears. "This stuff," she spluttered, lest they misunderstand, "is disgusting. When are you guys going to learn to make decent coffee?"

"It needs a woman's touch," said Avi.

"Don't we all?" Eli winked. "Why don't you move up here, Zara? Help us out with the coffee and all."

"Three meals a day with you guys is enough for me, thanks."

"Come on, we're not so bad. A little horny, maybe, but that's to be expected."

Nasty macho laughter. She smiled broadly and said, "Horny? Maybe I can help with that."

They weren't laughing anymore. Eli gasped and put his hand on her thigh. "You can?"

"Absolutely," she replied and, holding his eye, poured a glass of cold water into his lap.

Beni drove her over to the kibbutz, which was showing an American movie. Ronar was loitering outside, alone, when they arrived. He sat beside Zara. After the movie, Beni took her arm and said, "Come on, I'll drive you home."

"I'll take her," Ronar said quietly, with an unfriendly glance at Beni. The small man seemed about to argue, but Zara said, "No point in your taking me, Beni. Ronar's going up there anyway."

With a mournful look, Beni dropped her arm and walked

away. Zara felt guilty, decided she was meant to, and dropped it.

There were bats around them, so swift and silent that they were just a darkening of the air and a sensed presence. They appeared and disappeared without continuity.

When they got in the jeep, Ronar, staring forward, did not immediately start the jeep nor did he speak. Does he expect me to bring it up? she wondered indignantly, and said, "Not bad, the movie."

"Not bad," he mimicked.

"Do you want me to go to Nachal Arugot tomorrow? I haven't been for a while."

He had turned and was watching her. She's tough, he thought. Not a sign of jealousy or anger. No sign, either, of recognition. They were back to square one, and if he wanted her again he'd have to take the initiative and risk being rejected. Would the creature dare reject him? "Fine," he said.

He's cool, she thought. Not a sign of embarrassment. Why should there be? There were no promises, none even implied. And he's never been my man. Raif was—is.

"You missed a good scene at dinner tonight," she said as they drove along the Dead Sea, and she told him about Eli's crack and the glass of water. Then she laughed, self-satisfied, but Ronar replied grimly:

"I didn't miss it. If I'd been there, it wouldn't have happened." His anger surprised her until she figured out that he was jealous of his dominant position among the men. She was his worker, and they needed his permission to flirt with her.

"They asked where you were."

"What did you say?"

She looked at him, all innocent surprise. "Nothing. It's not my business."

It wasn't. Teaching her, that had been the whole point of the exercise. Why then was she scoring all the points? Ronar brooded.

When he stretched his arm along the jeep's backrest she stiffened, and he withdrew. Instead of stopping at her cabin he drove straight to his. That had been his silent signal for sex, saving him the commitment of even a euphemistic invitation. Before he could turn off the motor, she had said good night and swung her legs over the side. "Zara, wait." He grabbed her arm more tightly than intended. "Won't you come in?"

She wanted to ask, "Aren't you pushing it a bit?" but they weren't on such intimate terms. "I'm pretty tired," she said and went home.

The night was bad. He'd never lost sleep over a woman before but it wasn't her fault. As she joined him in the jeep to drive up for breakfast he said, "About that girl—"

"What girl?"

How the hell had she made it to the ripe old age of twenty-two? By rights someone should have knocked her off long ago. "The girl who was beneath me when you walked in yesterday. Don't raise your eyebrows at me. I'm just telling you that it doesn't matter. She doesn't matter."

"What do you mean, it doesn't matter? I almost missed dinner last night. Next time please leave a note."

Let her take her best shot. It didn't bother him; her voice was shaking. "Maybe," Ronar said gently, "there won't be a next time."

Why the hell not? she wondered fiercely.

She hurt.

She had learned from her mother that you don't show

pain, ever. The best way was to turn pain into anger, but she couldn't hate Ronar. Hatred was for enemies, like Uri, and traitors, like her mother. Ronar was not an enemy, and having made no promises he could break none. She knew she didn't love him because she loved Raif. Still, mysteriously, she hurt, and like an undiagnosed disease her pain was frightening.

For comfort she dredged up the old litany, and repeated it: Who's this Ronar anyway? Just Raif's stand-in, Raif's ice-cold shadow. Ronar's not real.

But if he wasn't, his absence was. Days, weeks passed, and she was alone. Remoteness attacked from without: distances seemed uncrossable, voices far away, the desert hostile, her work futile. Despair, like a disembodied spirit, fought for possession of her body, which responded with a burst of sexual starvation. She was ravenous—but her body rejected all the men she tried to feed it.

She let Beni walk her down to the shore one evening after dinner, defying Ronar's scowl. Of course he embraced her. But his kiss was sticky and his smell was strange, and before she knew it she had pushed him away. The soldiers about were too young and their officers too military. There were always tourists. She could have had a tourist, meant to, decided to, but somehow didn't get around to it.

Ronar came upon her in Nachal David, leaning against a tree, staring into space. When she noticed him he was right beside her, laughing soundlessly. "Is this what I pay you for?"

"Sorry, I just . . ."

"It won't do, Zara. Come to my room after dinner." She watched him walk away. Those long, even strides, that fluid body. Mr. Fucking Ein Gedi. Was he going to fire her?

At dinner she sat far away. Once in a while she felt a

warm, immaterial touch, and looked up to see his eyes on
her. No smile; but if he didn't want her, she'd eat her
badge.

She put on clean clothes and went to his cabin. This time
she knocked. He opened the door, pulled her inside.
Kicking the door closed behind them, he turned her head up
and kissed her. Her arms closed around him. With his lips
still on hers he carried her into the bedroom and laid her on
the bed. There were no preliminaries and no conversation.
When they were finished Zara said, "I thought you were
going to fire me."

"No, you can stick around for a while."

"Thanks, boss." And she went home to sleep.


Few, very few, letters came from Raif. She had lived in
Ein Gedi for nearly two years when she received the third.
Beni gave it to her at breakfast, but it was not until siesta
that she was left alone to read it. Then, lying in her bed in
the utter silence of the afternoon, she read:

> "My love Zara,
>
> Muhammed is getting out tomorrow so I'm giving
> him this for you. It's better if even he doesn't know
> who I'm writing to, so I'll send it through Rachamim,
> as usual.
>
> But really I have little to say, too little perhaps to
> justify the harm I do us both by writing. The days are
> all alike, all gray, so it's hard to tell one from another,
> or to tell time. Time for me is only the passage
> between one thought of you and the next. Outside of
> my thoughts the emptiness and the stink of prison life
> surround me, and were it not for thoughts of you I
> would be absorbed and dissolved. Already I'm not

what I was, and every day I lose more. As each part of me dies I forget that it ever was, and all that remains are impressions of loss. If I get out I will no longer know how to walk in the sun.

You don't exist for me anymore, except as a thought and a memory. I would be astonished to find that you still have a body and a voice, you have become so mistified in me. Only your letters convince me that there is a real Zara corresponding to my fantasy one. In a way it's not so important any more. But it's to her, the real Zara, that I'm trying to speak now. I have a message, from beyond.

Don't wait, Zara. Nothing is more destructive than waiting, take that from one who has nothing else to do. I don't need you to wait. It's the image of Zara I need, and I have that. What comes out of this prison will not be what went into it, and I don't want your eyes there to register the change.

That concludes the noble, self-sacrificing part of my message to you, Zara. Now stop reading, because what I feel coming next is weak and all wrong. ·

Wait for me, Zara. Don't ever stop thinking of me —because it's your thoughts of me, not mine of you, that sustain me.

I'm sorry. I didn't want to lay that on you. Only to tell you, my love, that wherever you go my love is upon you, forever. You be the carrier of our freedom.

Raif."

She was late for work. Ronar knocked and when no answer came opened her door.

She lay with her back to the door, corpse-rigid. The single ray of light that entered through the shuttered window fell across her clenched hands. Ronar could see only the side of her face, set in a dry paroxysm of grief, a tragic mask.

He diagnosed either a scorpion sting or snake bite, and leaped across the room. When he saw her fists clutching her stomach as though staunching a wound, he was sure she'd been bitten in the abdomen. Ignoring the sudden weakness that ran through him, he pulled her hands away and bent to search for the puncture.

Zara, who had not heard him enter, was at first astonished. Then she understood, and said dryly, "I'm all right. Leave me alone."

He straightened, and his eyes fell on the letter in her fist and on its flowing Arabic script. Seeing this, she hardened herself for the rejection that was sure to come. Instead, he acted in a way that made no sense to her. Silent as always, he lay on her narrow bed beside her, enfolded her in his arms, and just held her. It was the first noncoital embrace he'd ever given her, the first, though she did not know it, he'd given any woman.

His tenderness amazed her as much as if the mountains themselves had laid soft hands on her. She turned into his embrace, and he fitted his body to hers. Always when they made love he entered from behind, or braced himself above her. But now the coolness of his body, like the desert dusk, soothed all the heated length of hers.

Later she knew it was an aberration, like rain in August, a sweet delusion. He hadn't meant it. True comfort came from Ein Gedi itself, from the balance of the oasis poised on the desert's edge. The clearest lines of demarcation in the world ran through Ein Gedi, like the border of the dead salt sea and the desiccated shore, or the lines of dawn and sunset, when the temperature rose or fell by twenty degrees within minutes, or the sudden passage from arid rocky hills to plush green wadis. It soothed her to find, so predictably, scorpions and snakes on the heights, soft plump mammals and tropical birds in the valleys. Such lines and balance, intrinsically valuable, were apart from and above the imbalance and muddy imperfection of human affairs.

One day, a month later, she traveled to Be'er Sheva with Ronar, who had a meeting in the Reserve Authority offices. On her way to the used bookstore there was an art supplies shop. With no conscious intent, she entered it.

Never having drawn or painted before, she had no idea of what to buy. Finally she settled for a sketch pad, a set of colored pencils, and watercolors.

Hurrying back to the empty jeep, she hid her purchases under the seat. The next time Ronar sent her to work alone in Nachal Arugot, she wore a knapsack. Ronar noticed but, reliably, asked no questions.

Sketching the hidden waterfall was meant to be a joke on herself. How could she, who could not portray the most patiently posing rock, hope to capture a waterfall? But a strange thing occurred, when she came down to it. Her head grew silent, her eyes filled with the falls, and her hand drew lines. And when she was through, she looked down, and saw that she had not captured anything, but that something was growing on the pad.

# CHAPTER III

Yoav was the closest thing to a friend that Ronar had, and Zara's enemy. No amount of desert stupefaction could block out her inherent bristling response to his political smell, nor his to hers. Yoav worked for the Nature Authority, but belonged to their infamous political arm, the Green Patrol. The main function of this was the removal of Bedouin inhabitants from Reserve land.

Ronar's authority was inborn, but Yoav's was external —he preferred to display his holstered on his hip or strapped to the inside of his jeep. He wore his curly black hair close-cropped under a visored army cap and, below that, a string of beads and one gold earring. This effect was balanced by his ever-present revolver and a habitual, malicious glint in his eyes. The Bedouin called him Goat.

He'd fought with Ronar on the Golan front in '67; that was all she knew. Ronar never talked about the war, and she wasn't allowed to question him. And questioning Yoav about the war meant listening to his self-glorifying boasts (of all the seduction plays she'd encountered, the most obnoxious) and to his vociferous hatred for Arabs.

Even if he had not reeked of racism, she would have been compelled to hate him because he threatened her. They first met several months after Zara came to work on the Reserve. Up in Nachal Arugot, she discovered signs that someone was camping and building fires near one of the upper pools. After work, she went straight to Ronar's cabin to report. Yoav was there, and she knew at once, by Ronar's relaxed air, that the two men had a history. Ronar's voice was nearly jovial, introducing them. The small man looked her over deliberately, his eyes black with malicious knowledge. For a long moment she feared that Ronar had been mocking her to him. But the stranger said thoughtfully, "Zara. I've heard that name recently. Some dirty affair up north. Escapes me at the moment though. It'll come back."

Ronar glanced curiously at her. She imagined, was meant to imagine, her expulsion from Ein Gedi: marched out by a cold-eyed Ronar while her companions turned their backs. Nobody likes an Arab-lover. She wanted to run; but Yoav was a snake, and his slithering words were meant to startle. So she leaned against a wall, lit a cigarette, and smiled. For a moment, she looked extraordinarily like her mother.

"It'll come back," he repeated and turned to Ronar, blotting her out. "Had any good ones lately, Ronar? I picked up this American tourist the other day, sixteen, maybe seventeen years old and ripe, man, hitching down to Eilat. First I order her into the car, see, then I show her my badge. The cunt can't read Hebrew of course, so she thinks I'm a cop. I give her the lecture, you know, the dangers of hitching alone and all that crap, and threaten to lock her up for her own good. Pretty soon she's crying and begging me to go easy on her. That's when I lay it on her. 'You wanna do something for a war hero?' I says—"

Zara left.

It was Yoav who, eighteen months later, brought the orders from Jerusalem to evict the Bedouin shepherds and their families from the newly confiscated Reserve land south of Ein Gedi.

He wasn't a snake. He was a political disease and a carrier of political disease. His catalytic visits smudged the perfect clarity of the desert, and infused Zara with doubt and the fear that Ein Gedi was not a solution but a particularly fragile suspension.

He told Ronar, and Ronar told Zara, driving up to dinner at the Field School. "They've decided," Ronar said, "to expand the Reserve to Wadi Darage in the south and north to the edge of the kibbutz."

"Does that mean you're going to throw out the Bedouin?"

"It means we are."

She thought she'd said nothing but must have said no. He glanced down at her and said flatly, "You'll help. It's the price you pay for living here."

She had never argued with him. Now she dared to say, "Are you going to tell Mustapha to take his family and his goats and get out? He's lived here longer than you."

Ronar pulled over, stopped the jeep. She had an idea he might hit her, though he didn't look mad. The sun had just set behind the mountains, and she kept her eyes on their immaculate silhouettes. Something dangerous was rising.

"There are other places for the Bedouin," Ronar said calmly.

"Sure, fucking Bedouin reservations. The army grabs a piece of the Negev, the kibbutzim expand, and now we're taking our pound of flesh." Her voice was shaking.

"What do you care?" His was merely curious.

Lava flowed through her veins and into her mouth. When she spoke, it spilled onto him. "That's just like you. Of course you don't care. How could you? You have nothing to care with, no feelings. I think of you as a robot, and I'm amazed at how consistently you confirm it. You're just like your precious Nature Reserve, untouchable. I'd call you a human Reserve except that I query the 'human.' "

"Zara."

" 'Don't step off the trail, don't pick the flowers, and for God's sake don't plant anything.' That's you."

"No," he said.

"No? Then how come, Ronar, when you fuck me I feel like I'm the one who's trespassing?"

He put the jeep in gear and drove. He answered nothing, and it would have taken better eyes than hers to read that stony face; but her unwanted sense chose that moment to intrude on her certainty. She heard him think: You feel only what you want to feel. That was true, but not hermetically so; for against her will she felt his pain. But for the first time in her life, she discounted information so received as too unlikely to be true.

All through dinner the Ein Gedi crew discussed the expulsion order, speculating about what had led to the decision. Dan, the American guide, naïvely assumed that no other solution to the black goat problem could be found. Beni, apathetic to the reasons, expressed fierce satisfaction that soon the area would be Arab-free. Certainly no one was unhappy. In a Jewish state, it was implied, the Arab may be grateful for whatever tolerance he gets.

When she could no longer contain herself, Zara interrupted. "Look," she said. "If you're wondering why, if you want to get at the purpose behind any political decision,

look at whose interest it serves." Ariella's Law, she called
it. She noticed Eli, across the table, gaping at her, felt a
noncommittal watchfulness in the other men. "The Bedouin
are being taken off their land, which means a larger
percentage of privately owned land remains in Jewish
hands, and therefore a larger slice of the economy. They're
moved to reservations near Jewish development towns and
given just enough land to build a house, but, and here's the
point, not enough to work a subsistence living. If they don't
want to starve, they must take jobs. And where will they
find jobs? Where else but in the development towns! And
not only the men, because Arab children come very cheap.
So we're left with cheap Arab labor for Jewish industrialists
and concentration of land in Jewish hands, and you can take
it that those were the goals of whoever is behind this
scheme."

As a black mood settled on the men, she felt a surge of
hope that she had touched them. But then an angry chorus
of protests broke out, and she knew the only place she'd
moved them was against her. Eli raised his voice above the
others and demanded: "How can you say such things?" Not,
she thought sadly, how could they be, but how could you
say them? She retorted, "How can you pretend not to know
them already?"

"What's not to know? The only question is, whose side
are you on?"

The question echoed in the suddenly silent room, till
Ronar, seeing that she did not intend to reply, said quickly,
"One thing's wrong with your analysis. We're taking land
for the Reserve, not for Jewish farmers."

Zara shrugged, burnt out. It changed nothing, Ronar's
point; the effect was too finely directed and too clearly

perceived. But it would do no good to argue with her peers in ineffectuality.

That evening, Ariella was so much on her mind that it was almost no surprise to open her door to a knock and find Ariella standing there. The two women gazed at each other, then embraced warmly.

"You've come about the Bedouin?" Zara said.

Ariella nodded, lit a cigarette, and leaned back on Zara's bed, looking curiously around the bare room. "I was their lawyer. The Lost Cause Madonna, they're calling me."

"So you've come down to share defeat."

She shrugged. "It's better to have witnesses here. They won't resist, but the pigs get off on rough evictions. Do you know this place looks like a cell?"

No, she only knew it felt good. "Who's doing it?"

"The fucking Green Patrol. Not Ronar, thank God."

"What's the difference? We all work for the Nature Reserve Authority, so we're all responsible."

"They're puppets, Zara. They're just letting themselves be used."

"Is that supposed to comfort me? Are you saying it's okay to let yourself be used?"

Ariella was silent. Damned if she was going to send this girl into battle again. She considered herself hard, with all the armor necessary to a warrior. But this one got beneath it, never meaning to but reaching straight into her sheltered wells of pity and love, wells she'd sealed when her own infant daughter died.

"I know I should resist, or leave. But where would I go, Ariella? Are the Bedouin going to give me a home if I join their exile? Are you going to find me another haven? They don't last long."

"You don't have to," Ariella said gently, knowing she

was wrong. It was bad advice; Zara would pay for her passivity. But still she said comfortingly, "What would it profit them?"

"Hey, Ariella, you taught me better than that. I know that's not the point. This is a funny Garden of Eden. The guilty stay; and the innocent get driven out."

Here was something, perhaps, she could teach Zara, an attitude that buffered the heads of those compelled to butt; it was something she could not formulate, but only display. Smiling with her bottom lip, frowning with her upper, Ariella said, "Look at it this way. The process is elegant. Putting it through the Reserve Authority was a stroke of genius. 'We're not persecuting the Bedouin, we're saving the ecology.' Naturally, the Israeli public is more concerned with saving a nice vacation spot than with destroying the Bedouin's livelihood. Afterward, of course, they'll quietly turn the confiscated land over to the kibbutz, to raise their fucking Jewish goats."

Zara was shocked. "Ronar would cut off his balls before he'd help the kibbutz!"

"He doesn't believe it will happen."

"Well, how do you know it will?"

"Common sense, experience, not hard evidence. Just wait, and you'll see it happen."

"I love Ein Gedi," Zara said. "If the Bedouin are to be thrown out anyway, then better the land should go to the Reserve. We'll keep the spoilers out. Maybe someday the Bedouin will be back."

"Zara, you've chosen to stay, and perhaps you're right to stay. But do it with open eyes, please. The Bedouin are never going to come back here. Look at it, if you will, as a historical spectacle: someone ought to sell tickets. I can hear the barkers now: 'Ladies and gents, so you missed the slaughter of the American Indians? Never mind, step right up, you're right on time for the annihilation of the Bedouin!' "

It drew a rueful smile from Zara.

"Where are you staying, lady?"

"With the Bedouin."

For all your words, Zara thought but, emulating Ariella, said, "A ringside seat, huh? You are greedy!"

On the day of the eviction, Zara drove down to the Bedouin camp with Ronar.

Ten flat trucks and a small bus had been provided to move the dozen extended families. Their tents were down, their possessions crated, the goats were penned, ready to be moved. Each Bedouin family squatted by its bundles. The living encampment, deflated, had been turned into a still-life of incipient exile. Zara remembered a scene she'd never seen, a bequeathed memory of Jews huddled in a town square, guarding their bundled possessions while loud-speakers blared impeccably alphabetized names. A ring of soldiers surrounded the square, while townspeople peeped from behind curtained windows. Some wore on their faces a look that Zara now felt on her own, a look of pity and truculent shame.

Leaving the jeep, Zara wandered up to Mustapha, con-quering an urge to hide her face from him. She couldn't speak until his voice released her.

"Come to say good-bye, Zara?" Although his Hebrew was excellent, they always spoke Arabic. He sounded kind: she wondered that he could have sympathy to spare.

"To say good-bye, and I'm sorry, and ashamed. I know it's useless to say."

"Not entirely useless. And I think you have no need to be ashamed. It is not your doing."

Mustapha's daughter, Alia, came over to them. A year or two older than Zara, she had a five-year-old son and an infant girl, now sleeping at her breast. She told Zara, "Your friend Beni drove over this morning. He came to my father and told him, 'This is Jewish land now.' My father said, 'How can the land be Jewish? Land has no religion.' Zara, is that what the Jews believe? I think your people must be mad, or very primitive indeed to believe such nonsense. And stupid, Zara, very stupid. Because if through a miracle Allah gave voice to the land, it would surely tell us that it belongs to no people, but that people belong to the land. And if any people belong to the desert, it is the Bedouin."

Patiently, Mustapha told his girl, "It is not religion, only politics and greed. The Israelis make the law, and they make it decree that the land the Bedouin live on is Israeli land. Only they disguise their motives. It is never for political reasons, no; it is security, or the social good, or conservation, or it is because they want to civilize the primitive Bedouin. The boundaries of the Jews' humanitarian confiscations form a pen to imprison the Bedouin, who do not even pen their goats."

There came the sound of a jeep driven dangerously fast. With a rifle by his side and pistol at his waist, Yoav drove into camp, a false Lone Ranger in a cloud of dust. Ten meters away, he braked, and barked out Mustapha's name. The old man loked up impassively.

"Mustapha, you fucking Arab bastard, get over here. I've come all the way from Be'er Sheva because of you."

In a voice as cold as desert night, Mustapha answered, "If you've come so far to see me, Goat, you can get out of there and walk another few meters over here."

He left Yoav with a choice of two ways of losing face.
He could continue the shouted conversation, or he could
walk over. Yoav had a high-pitched voice which grew
higher when he shouted, until he sounded like a boy. He left
the jeep and swaggered over to Mustapha, carrying his rifle.

"What the hell are all these dogs doing here?" he
demanded. "You're moving into decent government hous-
ing. You people can't bring these infested curs along."

Mustapha spoke slowly. "The government said we could
bring our livestock. These dogs work, they herd the goats.
They come with us."

Zara glanced around surreptitiously, looking for Ronar.
He was far away, and Yoav was raving, climaxing on his
authority.

"Don't tell me about government orders, you cheeky
bastard. I told you, no dogs!" He swung around, raising his
rifle. One of the dogs who'd been dozing in the shadow of
the jeep was startled by the sudden movement and jumped
up. Yoav aimed and squeezed off a shot. It lifted the dog,
slammed him against the jeep, and then dropped him onto
the ground, a bloody dead mess. A child screamed. Yoav
wheeled, sighted another dog and shot. This time he caught
it in the hindquarters. The dog was crippled and bleeding
profusely, but not yet dead. It screamed continuously. Yoav
left it alive, in agony, and ran around the camp, shooting at
dogs. Women, shrieking in terror, made grabs for their
children, pushing them under their skirts. Mustapha made a
move toward Yoav, but the ranger pointed the rifle at him
and toyed with the trigger.

Alia's five-year-old had a Canaani pup that he adored.
When the puppy squirmed out of his arms, the child broke
free of his mother to chase his pet. Yoav had already taken
aim when the boy caught up and threw himself over the

puppy. Over the mother's scream, Ronar's voice broke like thunder: "Yoav! Don't!" There was a frozen moment, while Yoav held the rifle lined up with the boy's head. Through the corner of her eye Zara saw Alia sink to her knees on the sand, covering her face but watching through split fingers. Then, casting a filthy look back at Ronar, Yoav slung the rifle over his shoulder, ran over and tossed the child, still clutching his dog, into the jeep, then jumped in and drove toward the hills.

Alia laid her infant on the ground, caught up her skirt, and ran silently, swiftly after the jeep, followed by her husband and Ariella. Ronar ran toward his jeep, but Zara got there first and ignoring his shouts she drove after Yoav. She heard him but, in the space she was in, his voice couldn't reach her.

Yoav stopped a kilometer away, out of sight but in easy earshot of the Bedouin camp. Pinning the child down with his boot, he wrested the dog away from him, tossed it out of the jeep, and shot it in midair. When Zara reached them, the boy was huddled in a fetal position on the floor of the jeep, waiting his turn.

"*Cusemach*," she cursed, vaulting to the ground, "they're going to hear that shot and think you've killed the child."

"Let them." Smiling, he stepped down to meet her. Zara kicked, aiming for his balls, but he sidestepped her. "Naughty, Zara."

What maddened her was his smile, his filthy enjoyment. Possessed by loathing but weaponless, she struck out with her fists and had the satisfaction of seeing his grin wiped away by her first hard blow to his belly. He backed off; she smelled his fear but fear was not enough. Her body held no room for pain or fear, no feeling but lust: his spirit was untouchable but she longed to flay his flesh. Zara, no debutante, fought like a street-fighting man; no hair pulling or polite scratchings in her repertoire, only kicks, low body blows, and face gouging. They rolled on the ground like lovers, Yoav the stronger, but unable to match her passion. Finally, pushing on top, he reared back and punched her in the breast. As her grip loosened, he jumped up and kicked her viciously in the head.

She was conscious but too dazed to move. The midday heat rose in waves from the burning sand. She watched him slowly, through the haze, draw his pistol, cock it, aim. He said, "Arab-loving cunt, here you go." She heard a shot, but felt no pain; and Yoav fell.

From far away, she heard Ronar call her name. Then he was beside her.

Later she understood that it was Ronar who fired. Running after Yoav, he had paused to take a gun from one of the soldiers supervising the eviction. He had feared that Yoav might be mad enough to shoot the child; and though he never said it, Zara believed that, had he done so, Ronar would have killed him summarily. As it was, he had come into range just in time to stop Yoav from shooting Zara.

They put Yoav, who was wounded in the arm, into one jeep, which Ronar drove to the kibbutz clinic. Zara was helped into the other by Ariella, where Alia and her husband were thawing their frozen child. After dropping them off, Ariella took Zara home, put her to bed, brought ice for her swelling face, kissed her, and said gruffly, "You did good, kid." Zara had been deeply shamed by Alia's abject gratitude; for she knew that the child had been nowhere in her mind when she fought Yoav. It was Raif she fought for, and revenge. A child of the region was Zara.

# CHAPTER IV

Zara dreamed that she was dining with her mother in an elegant restaurant sparkling with crystal, silver, and snow-white linen. White-gloved waiters hovered solicitously, and the kitchen must have been soundproofed. It was the kind of place Zara knew only from movies; not American movies, but European. The restaurant was, however, strangely located, deep in a desert wilderness, amidst dead-looking ash-gray mountains; and though perhaps a surrounding wall of some kind, to separate the inhabitants of this luxurious compound from the common people, would not have been incongruous, the electrified, double-strand, barbed-wire fence did seem a bit excessive. German shepherd dogs lay about the outside of the restaurant, gnawing bones tossed to them from the kitchen.

At the table, their order was taken by the headwaiter, who seemed to be an acquaintance of Zara's mother. The menu was divided into ethnic categories, and Zara was surprised to see a section of Bedouin dishes, including

Bedouin soup, Bedouin fricassee, liver, and steak tartare. She had not realized that there was a distinct Bedouin cuisine, much less that it was sophisticated enough to be included in such an exalted menu. The waiter recommended the pâté: "The materials we must use are primitive, Madam, but I think you'll find the dishes admirably executed. And may I suggest for your entrée, the specialty of the house?"

"What is it?" Ruth asked.

"It changes, Madam, from season to season."

"Fine, I'll try it," Ruth declared, and at once Zara was seized from behind by two burly men wearing chef's hats. As she was dragged screaming to the kitchen, she heard her mother cry: "But that's my daughter! That's my Hope!"

"Sorry, Madam," giggled the waiter, "no substitutions."

During the week that followed the land confiscation, Zara suffered two days of headache and a reprimand from Ronar. He came to her room late that first night, switched on the light, and removed the compress from her head to check the bruise. It was impressive: blue and swollen, ragged and red-rimmed where Yoav's boot had broken her skin. Zara smiled nervously.

"You should see the other guy. . . ."

Unsmiling and cold, Ronar said, "See the kibbutz doctor tomorrow."

"Yes, sir!"

He went to the door, hesitated, and came back. His eyes burned in a stone face; and in his voice was anger but also a kind of rusty generosity. "Was that," he asked, "the best you could do?"

"What are you telling me? What should I have done?"

"Except under the greatest provocation, Yoav would

never hit a woman. You should have used that to get the child away from him."

"I didn't want to use that. It never occurred to me—I didn't want to be thought of as a woman by him."

"If you weren't prepared to use your sex, then you should have gone ready to beat him on a man's ground. But you didn't do that either. You chased an armed man unarmed, and started a fight with a man you knew could beat you."

"I didn't even think of winning, Ronar. I just wanted to hurt him."

He touched her bruise with a hand as gentle as his face was hard. "Don't you ever think of the cost?"

"I'm no accountant."

"No. But you're not a very effective fighter either."

If he'd searched for years, he could have found nothing to say that would have hurt her more.

In fact, though he pretended anger, he could not think badly of her. Her faults were pride and an excess of courage which, though stupid, was true. They were not the kind of faults he could despise.

Ronar never raised the matter again, but she learned from Beni that Yoav had lost his job. Because of the child? she asked. No, she was told, because of what he did to you, and what he almost did.

She was content, and her guilt about the Bedouin dissolved with the punishment of Yoav. All week they labored on the fence which was to enclose the new area of the Reserve; with every stake hammered into the ground Zara's heart sang: There's one for the endangered species! There's one for the exiles! After work, Ronar and Zara drove through their new protectorate, leaving the jeep, when it could penetrate no farther through the narrow wadis and steep mountain trails, to explore on foot the land they had inherited. If the Bedouin, so unjustly removed, had been of the land, then so would they be. As they rode and walked through his new domain, Ronar disposed: here they would irrigate and plant grass for the ibex, here they would clear a trail up the mountain, here they would place pitons for intrepid hikers, and this perfect spot would be off limits to all but Reserve personnel—the king and his consort.

They had one week of this, no more. Sunday morning at breakfast, Beni handed Ronar a letter from the Reserve Authority that blackened his face as he read it. No one dared ask what it contained, but when he tossed it down contemptuously and strode from the room, Beni read it aloud. The land which had been taken from the Bedouin had been made over to the Ein Gedi kibbutz, "effective immediately."

Humiliation she felt, perfect humiliation. Better have been caught naked in a roomful of strangers than in such a gross political naïveté. Was she born yesterday, to be so taken in? Had she sold out her convictions, her conscience, for the fat-assed kibbutzniks? No, she had acquiesced in thievery in order to enjoy the spoils. Now the goods were being taken away from her, and what a bloody fool she was.

She didn't see Ronar again until late that night. Walking along the dirt road toward the kibbutz in the familiar dark, she heard a jeep approaching and thought of hiding but didn't. It stopped in front of her. Pinned in the glare, she knew him only by his growl. "Get in," Ronar said, and she obeyed.

He looked her over. "I warned you about this."

She heard expulsion in his tone and quavered, "What?" She had no idea of what he was about to say. Was he offering her a lift, taking her home, or throwing her out? For all she knew he could be arresting her.

"This stupid lack of preparation." She sank into his scorn

like the softest of pillows. "You dilettante, what harm could you do with those?" and he flicked her wireclippers. "Or did you only want to 'hurt' the fence?" He, she saw now, had loaded the jeep with a generator, an electric saw, and empty wire spools.

"They'll hear," she ventured timidly, and he smiled fractionally.

They had dismantled half the fence bordering on the kibbutz when the jeepload of kibbutzniks drove up. Four men alighted, holding guns which they put aside as they recognized Ronar.

The kibbutz secretary approached them and demanded to know what the hell they were doing; Ronar answered tersely, "You've got eyes, Landau."

"And you've got fucking nerve. This is kibbutz land now."

"Yes, but the fence is ours. I'm taking it home." He switched on the saw and bent to his work. The kibbutznik moved forward; but as he did Ronar straightened and turned, and the blade turned with him. Landau stopped and blustered: "Are you threatening me?"

"No, man. I'm taking my fence home."

They crowded together, herd animals, threatening and cursing over the buzz of the saw, while Ronar saved his breath for his work and Zara stood behind him, coiling the wire as he cut each strand free. So long as none came within range of his saw, Ronar ignored them. Then Landau walked toward Ronar's jeep.

"Don't touch that generator, Landau." Ronar's voice was mild, but the kibbutznik froze. "I had some trouble hooking it up to the saw. If you touch it while this tool is on, you'll get the shock of your life."

When at last they gave up and drove away, Ronar

switched off the saw and turned to Zara. The quarter moon softened the jagged planes of his face, and his unaccustomed smile gave him a momentary look of pure and youthful delight. He pulled her to him, and she sensed him, for the first time, hard on the outside, soft inside.

Later that night, after they had made love, and she had lain long enough for the sweat to dry on her body, Zara moved to go. "Stay," Ronar said quietly, "stay. I'm going to want you in the morning."

Obediently, she did. He slept with a hand on her breast while she watched through the night and into the dawn. Sounds grew clearer, as they often do at night: so clear that she could hear the wolves howling though there were none in Ein Gedi.

It came over the radio at dinner that Raif was dead. In the midst of the coffee-slurping, dish-clattering, raunchy-joking clamor of the field school kitchen, the words pierced her so cleanly that at first no one noticed she'd been hit. The announcer's tone was faintly triumphant.

"Arab prisoners in Ramle prison rioted today following the killing of an Arab inmate, allegedly at the hands of a group of Jewish inmates. The Arab, Raif Hawill, was stabbed in his cell by what police described as numerous homemade knives fashioned from eating utensils. No motive for the stabbing was revealed, and police have not ruled out a political motive. The Arab rioters have been subdued and returned to their cells."

Why did she feel nothing? Was there nothing to feel? No, there was a great deal to feel; there was a crushing black cloud of feeling waiting just beyond the boundaries of her perception. Was it, then, that her sensors were dead? It seemed so, for even vision was gone, and internal static drowned out all outside sound. And her thoughts for once were so airy, so detached and spacious, as if she experienced the bliss of the instantly beheaded.

Then, like receding waves, silence and blackness drained away, and voices rose to her ears. They were remote; but she could identify the sources and see the faces flickering through the grayness. She focused on Beni, whose face, across the table, was turned aside to his neighbor. Even in profile she recognized the playful, beguiling smile he used on her. He was saying, "But seriously, I do admire those guys. They may be murderers, rapists, thieves, the Jewish drek of the world. But when it comes down to brass tacks, they're still patriots. And they've got guts to do what our fucking government is too weak to do: wipe out the terrorist scum."

She had nothing against Beni, even thought him, in her distant way, a friend. And, content to be where she was, out beyond the pain barrier, she didn't want to react. But, simply, there are some words and some bodies that cannot share the same space. Zara's body picked up her cup, filled it to the brim with steaming coffee, and splashed it into Beni's face.

Ronar long remembered it as the most graceful act he'd ever seen, and he a secret collector of grace.

Beni screamed. He pulled up his shirt and wiped his face. He opened his eyes and through a mist of tears saw Zara, empty cup in hand.

She moved with the perfect, thoughtless fluidity of an animal. Showing no sign of emotion she stood and backed slightly away from the table, her knife seeming to flow from sheath to hand. When Beni didn't immediately attack, she mimed uncertainty and fear, with just the drop of a shoulder, the shift of an eye, to draw him on.

Oh, she was mad, mourned Ronar, and how was it that only at this moment of discovering how lost she was did he know how badly he wanted to reach her? He knew her story, had known it from the start, when Ariella, to gain shelter for the girl, had confided in him. Clearly, she was behaving like a doe drawing a hunter from her fawn. But Zara's fawn was already dead.

Beni, enraged by pain, had risen and was stalking her. Zara didn't move. Wondering at the reckless depth of her self-exposure, Ronar checked the expressions of the other men in the room. The taste for blood was manifest in them all. He understood. For two years she had controlled her body like private land and, worse than refused, had ignored their blandished courtships, had turned back their scouting patrols. They'd allowed her her autonomy. But now that she'd branded herself hostile Arab territory, they were hot and righteous for invasion.

He stood up and quietly moved to stand beside her.

She didn't notice him until Beni's stride faltered, and his eyes shifted focus. Then she turned, and the look she laid on Ronar held nothing of gratitude. But Ronar, old animal handler that he was, firmly grasped her arm and propelled her from the room. Her body, pushed where it did not want to go, lost its celestial grace and became ponderous and awkward. He loaded her into the jeep like a sack of grain.

Ronar, no accountant either, couldn't calculate the deficits involved in keeping her, nor the odds that he could do so. An attack by the heart was the only attack against which he had no ready defense, except to call his feeling, pride of possession. He felt a desperate tenderness for Zara in her pain, and a desire beyond all others to shelter her from further harm. But there was a sadness built into the realization, for Zara was like a stupid bird, who would not be consoled for the loss of a wing, but would keep struggling to fly on one.

He had no anger for what she had done to him. Without meaning to, without even noticing, she'd destroyed his peace and made him need her.

In his cabin he said to her, "You'll stay here with me. I'll go get your things."

But she didn't seem to hear. "I'm going to Nachal Arugot for a while," she said.

"No."

"You can't stop me." Disdainfully.

"Then I'll go with you."

"No!"

"You can't go alone."

"If you try to come with me, I'll get away from you."

She could do it, he knew, for she'd learned all he knew about the canyon, and she was lighter and faster than he. Thinking of the accidents that befall distracted people in the wilderness, he considered physical restraint, but quickly rejected the idea. She was like him, and would never mourn before witnesses. And if she needed to wander alone through the dessert, well, some people have unusual life-support requirements, and it does no good to deny them.

"I love you, Zara." She stared narrowly at him, not believing it for a moment.

While she was gone, he did what he could to enable her to stay. During dinner the next night, he announced conversationally, "The matter's buried. Anyone who wants to dig it up is going to have to talk to me. Anyone who lays a hand on her will regret it."

Beni said through pain-stiffened lips, "That goes for me, too."

Eli was outraged. "After what she did to you? Have you looked in the mirror? They'll be calling you piebald for months, chump. You'll draw a lot of broads with that mug."

"Even burnt, it's better than yours. No, see, I thought it over. If that Arab was her man, then I figure she had a right to do what she did. Besides, I admire her courage."

"What courage? She knew Ronar would stand up for her." Eli refused to look at Ronar, who said pleasantly, "When she threw that coffee, she didn't know I was alive."

Just outside the kitchen, Eli caught up with Ronar and said, "We'll let her stay on Beni's say-so, not yours, Superman. But I'll tell you one thing: that bitch is pure, pure trouble. One of these days she's gonna let it loose without you there to watch her back. And that," he spat, "will be the end of Zara."

Three nights after she went out, she came tapping at Ronar's door, asking for food. He let her in and fed her. As she devoured fresh bread and butter, cheese and fruit, he watched her, then looked away to say gruffly, "It's all right for you to stay."

She seemed surprised. "Oh, I'm not staying. I've got to go back to Tivon for a while. Then I'm going abroad."

He'd never thought of pleading with a woman. Of all the people he despised, pussy-whipped men he held the lowest. Still he would have done something had he seen the smallest opening in her eyes. But, watching her eat hungrily, with more thought for the food than for him, he knew with certainty that among the factors she'd considered in making

her decision, he'd weighed nothing at all. In his humiliation, he let her go impassively, without a word of dissua-
sion.

Zara, seeing none of this, understood merely that the
cold-hearted desert man had finally, and rightfully, grown
tired of her. She hadn't dared hope for any impression of
pain. But, like a no-good Indian, she'd left a trail of
broken-twig intentions, and robbed herself even of his
surprise.

"When will you go?" he asked.

There is no special Hebrew word for "you" spoken to a
lover. But there was an isotropic difference in his saying of
it that caught at Zara's attention. She looked up, curiously.

"Tomorrow morning, on the bus. I'm sorry to leave you
without a replacement."

Ronar shrugged to show that he'd done without her
before and would again. The letter he wrote a week later to
his wife, granting her her long-sought divorce, had nothing
to do with Zara.

# CHAPTER V

Not a face, not a house or a street or a smell had changed in Tivon, as if a spell had lain over the village. She passed the center—same woman selling flowers, same falafel kiosk, same old couple in the grocery. Only the fence was new, a barbed-wire perimeter surrounding the village, the modern equivalent, perhaps, of the impenetrable thorny hedge of fairy tale kingdoms. People nodded to Zara with the degree of attention due to one who has been away for a week. There was a distortion either in time, or her sense of it.

But, as if to compensate, the erosion in Rachamim was greater than the passage of two years could alone account for.

They sat in his Arab room. The windows to the wadi were shuttered, and despite the streaming sunlight outside, the room was dimly lit by a forty-watt bulb. By that light, the room which had seemed elegant and uncluttered, looked barren and poor. Rachamim asked her where she planned to go.

"Greece at first, Europe, maybe the States. I'm still an American citizen."

"You have money?"

"Two years' wages. There wasn't much to spend it on."

He nodded, then seemed to forget about her; his face settled into lines of such sadness that on a rare impulse of charity, she nearly invited him along. But greater than her sympathy was the desire, the need, to be unknown, to lose her past.

"How has the time passed for you, Rachamim?" she asked gently.

The face he let her see answered for him. Behind the eyes something was torn: internal bleeding showed in the desperate fragility of his coherence. He handled himself like eggshell china, and his voice, always soft, came out in a whisper.

"I've missed you both. None of the others come around anymore."

Two years ago, she'd been nearly carried out of there by Ariella, blind with hatred. Once her sight was restored she'd never looked back, never considered Rachamim, never wondered how he fared. It shook her to realize that while she'd thrived in the desert, he'd pined in the hills.

Really, nothing went as expected. She'd come back to haunt the town but found that, like most ghosts, she was invisible in her true form. What people saw was a self-engendered apparition: a good daughter of the village, come back from two years of rugged Zionist work in the desert to visit her old parents. No one, not a soul besides Rachamim, spoke Raif's name. It took her time to realize that this was meant, not as torment, but as forgiveness.

The morning after she arrived, Ruth came to Rachamim's house, drawn by rumor. It was midmorning, a Shabbat, and

Zara and Rachamim were drinking their second cups of coffee and talking quietly.

Zara stood up to meet her mother, eyes void and observant. Ruth touched her own cheek and said nervously, "I heard you were back." They gazed at each other over a distance neither moved to shorten.

"Hope," Ruth said.

"Zara," she corrected.

"Your father has heard that you're back. You'd better come home."

"How is he?" she asked, making of her politeness an offense.

"Not well."

"I'm sorry. And you?"

"Kind of you to ask how I am, after two years' silence."

"I knew I'd hear if either of you died," Zara explained. "And beyond that it really didn't matter."

Rachamim made a noise, a kind of bleeding laugh, and Zara said, in compunction, "Let's not do this here. I'll come over a little later."

Ruth left, and Rachamim apologized. "I couldn't invite her in. I'm sorry but I just can't have her under my roof."

"That's all right. I understand."

"No you don't. There's more to it. I didn't want to see the confrontation. You've gotten so hard, Zara. I hate your mother with a hate I never knew was in me. But seeing her faced with you—I actually pitied her."

"You think I am so bad?" she said in astonishment. "I only want to put things clearly."

"You've no idea what your kind of clarity does to people."

Her friend's charge of cruelty worked on her, moderating her behavior toward her parents. Come to haunt, she was received as a guest, and for a time allowed the pretense to continue. Somber Henry seemed almost gay as he talked, one whole evening, about his plans now that Zara had come home. They would be able to get some chicken coops, perhaps lay in a hothouse for roses. He asked for no confirmation, only rambled on as if afraid to stop. By ten o'clock he was nodding with exhaustion, and Ruth sent him, still talking, to bed.

In her straight-backed chair, hands folded tightly in her lap, Ruth was regal and dangerous. Her fierce black eyes pinned Zara to her place just as, years ago, they'd immobilized her while Ruth spun enmeshing visions. Now she said, "If you go abroad, you'll never see your father again. He's dying."

No sparrer, Zara observed, Ruth went straight for the knockout blow, which quick-footed Zara easily dodged and parried. "Then I'll tell him good-bye before I go."

It was a fair rejoinder, an honest blow; how unsporting of Ruth to exaggerate her pain so, flinching and crying out: "Where the hell do you come from?"

Zara began to laugh. "You know where, Mother."

"For his sake, you should stay."

"Impossible."

Ruth walked away, found a cigarette, lit it. When she turned back, her face was again composed and thoughtful. At fifty she was more herself than ever. Pride infused her. Zara loved her like an enemy.

"I know," Ruth was saying, "that I'm the reason you won't stay. Have you come here expecting an apology from me?"

"No."

"Good, because you'll never have one. I did what I had to do for both of us. Your understanding was and is unnecessary, and I'm certainly not in need of your forgiveness."

"I'm glad," said Zara simply, "because there's none in me to give."

It's true that it profited Zara to believe in her mother's indifference. But it's also true that Zara had little sense of other people's pain. Once there had been that cord through which feelings and thoughts flowed. But she'd pinched it shut. On the whole, it was better to feel orphaned than possessed.

She owed one courtesy call, but dreaded the paying of it. On her last visit to Dar Ayun, she'd been driven out with stones. But the thing could not be avoided.

Prudently she entered the village during the dog hours of the early afternoon. The streets were nearly empty except for an occasional old man drowsing outside a café or a woman carrying her day's shopping home on her head. Donkeys wandered unattended through the streets; dogs slept in the shade. Except for the sharp click of dice and backgammon pieces, and a low wailing song from a café radio, there was little to be heard. Glancing inside one café as she passed, Zara saw Daud playing backgammon with an older man. As she watched he sipped from a glass of Turkish coffee and threw the dice. He didn't see her, and she moved on.

She came to the house of Raif's parents, and knocked. His father answered. His face changed as he recognized her, but she could not read it. He glanced back at his wife, who nodded. Zara was admitted and offered a seat. Husband and wife sat opposite.

She offered her sympathy in formal terms, and formally they thanked her. Then she said, "I wonder if you can tell me what happened?"

"They say it was prison politics." The father's voice was not without pride. "They made Raif their victim because he was a leader of the Arab prisoners."

Had Raif grown political while she sheltered in the Reserve? Tentatively she said, "But outside he was never that fervent a nationalist. . . ."

"When they start slaughtering sheep, even lambs discover politics."

"And for *this* he was killed?"

Sensitive to her tone, Raif's mother spoke for the first time. "You are disappointed? You thought, perhaps, that he died because of you? How sad that we should shatter your romantic illusion. But better he should die for supporting his brothers than for loving a Jewish slut."

Raif's father made a sound of disapproval. Zara spoke to him as if she hadn't heard his wife's words.

"I don't understand. Outside he fought for coexistence. Couldn't he have continued there? Couldn't he have at least remained neutral?"

"Ramle prison is not Switzerland. There is no neutrality. Neutrality," and the taste of the word seemed bitter to him, "is for dogs, not men."

The streets were dead, the village moldered, and not even the dogs followed her progress through the empty town.

Almost all her classmates were married now, most living near Tivon. At the grocer's, she ran into Micha carrying an infant strapped to his back. He was wary and unsurprised and invited her for coffee.

Tsipi had gained weight; the rounded contours of her

olive-and-almond face were in the classic pattern of Mid-eastern beauty. Her sleek black hair was newly tailored, no longer waist length. Her manner was coolly polite.

The apartment seemed as if a battle between beauty and comfort had been waged and had ended in stalemate. The matching chairs were covered in a burlap-type material, and their wooden backs curved uncomfortably. Micha and Tsipi clung together on the sofa, sheltering behind a well-laden salon table. There was an arrangement of Formica shelves, with a few books, wedding and baby pictures, a stereo and records, and assorted decorative knickknacks.

They watched the news and, obliquely, Zara, until she began to feel like a feral animal, house-trained but not fully trusted, some kind of exotic cat perhaps. Etiquette demanded that she ask to see the baby, but she didn't dare, or didn't care to. After the news was over they turned off the television reluctantly, and conversed. First it was young couple topics: the baby, the apartment, the cost of everything. Zara was asked about Ein Gedi: what did she do, was it hard, how did she manage in the all-male society? It depressed her, sitting opposite old Micha, to have to strain their talk through his wife. It would have been good to argue with him one last time.

When they had exhausted the topic of Ein Gedi, and Zara could think of no questions for them whose answers were not self-evident, an awkward silence ensued; Micha broke it by saying with forced joviality, "Well, Zara, aren't you going to tell us about your boyfriend? I'm sure you haven't spent two years down there just for the scenery."

Zara closed her eyes. "Have you," she asked, too quietly, "forgotten who my 'boyfriend' is? Don't you remember?"

Tsipi offered more coffee and fled to the kitchen. Micha

was distressed. "I'm sorry—I thought we wouldn't talk about that."

"Why not? Is it too painful for you?"

"For me? No." He was simply puzzled, his passive complicity forgotten, though not by her. "Well, we thought you wanted a new start. That's why you came back, isn't it? Why rake up all that old mess?"

"That old mess," she repeated and felt, suddenly, too restless to wait for Tsipi and her coffee.

He walked her out. As she turned away he took her arm and said awkwardly, "Get yourself another man."

"Oh, are they interchangeable?"

"I'm telling you to settle down. You're living wrong. You make stupid choices."

Inside her burned a deep fire, and now it flared. She grabbed a handful of Micha's shirt and pushed her face up into his. "Settle down?" she mimicked. "Is that decent advice to give *me*? Settle down, have children, produce sons for the warrior-state? Live here, work here, pay taxes, donate blood whenever war comes? Why should I subsidize my enemies? No, Micha, never. I owe no allegiance and I'll have no state. To hell with homelands, to hell with a home."

"Then why have you come back?"

"Didn't it occur to you that I might have come back for revenge?"

"No," he said simply, "why should it? Are you a savage?"

She answered, "Yes." She knew what he meant.

All evening he'd watched her examine his apartment, his wife, his life with guarded eyes, eyes in which only he could read the thought, 'Here but for the grace of God go I.' How had he hoped for regret? Without maliciousness or even consciousness, without offering an alternative, she'd made his life seem futile, mean, and loveless in his own eyes. While she rode the wave of her passion recklessly to the end, though it threatened to break and leave her stranded on foreign shores, he had chosen to piddle about near the beach. He stood condemned of conventionality; but she was and remained in greater danger. She was not to be deflected; still he thought she heard him when he said, "Don't do anything irrevocable. Because someday, Zara, despite your 'never,' you may need to come home."

Rachamim was waiting up for her, leaning back on an ottoman, rolling a joint. On the floor beside him were four others, lined up. She sat beside him, shoulders touching. "What's this? Expecting company?"

"No." He handed her a joint and lit it. "How'd it go?"

"Strange." She inhaled, and started to pass the joint, but saw with some surprise that he'd lit one for himself. "It seems people imagine I came back to get married and settle down here."

He nodded, staring ahead. "And who do they expect you to marry?"

"They don't get specific. I suppose, as they see it, it doesn't really matter."

"Then you haven't heard," he looked at her now, "about us?"

"Us?" She inhaled badly and coughed. He wasn't laughing. "Are they really thinking that?"

"Of course. Why shouldn't they? You've been living here with me for over a week. You stayed here when Raif was busted. I'm fifteen years older than you, not exactly ancient. Who wouldn't assume I'm fucking you?"

Suddenly she was aware of his body, inches from hers,

lithe and young in tight jeans. Was this a prelude to a pass? A proposal? Why was he angry?

"Does it bother you," she asked cautiously, "what people think?"

"That's not it." Impatiently: "Zara, oh great truth-seeker, tell me: haven't you wondered?"

"What?" she said cravenly.

"Why I've never even tried to fuck you."

"No," she answered truthfully. "I never thought about it."

He looked at her sharply, then laughed in fond desperation. "That's very sweet. I know we're touching on your special area of stupidity, but try to consider it now. What do you come up with?"

She thought back. He had been an agent, never a principal, in the drama which starred Raif and herself. She could no more have considered Rachamim than Romeo could have left Juliet for the nurse. But who knew what lustful thoughts the nurse harbored? He would not have dared, she thought—but no, there had never been any sense between them of not daring, of reined passion. He just hadn't wanted.

"Because of Raif?" she ventured.

"Yes, because of Raif, but not the way you think." He lit another joint, and stared at it. "Not consideration for a friend, not respect for your feelings. All those weeks of the trial, and this past week, I haven't kept away from you for the sake of my friend's memory. There was, I'm afraid, no sacrifice involved.

"I never wanted you, Zara. I wanted him."

She felt not even a moment of disbelief, though she'd never thought of it. A memory arose. One spring day they'd gone on a hike, through the Judean desert. Starting at the low dry end of a wadi, they'd worked their way upward toward a water source. They came upon a ten-foot waterfall, a small deep pool at its foot. Shadowed by canyon walls, the water was freezing. The only way onward was to scale the wall beneath the waterfall. It was wet and slippery, but erosion had provided numerous hand and footholds. Rachamim went first, jumping into the water with his clothes on and clambering up the far wall, hugging the rock to avoid the water's force. Zara went next. The first time she made it halfway up before, turning to wave at Raif, she got hit broadside by the falling water and knocked back into the pool. The second try she reached the top, and Rachamim hauled her over the edge. Raif's climb was elegant, gravity-defying; Zara would hardly have been surprised if the waters had reversed direction to facilitate his passage. He accepted a hand from each of them to get over the side, and then stood there glistening and beautiful, water gleaming on his brown skin and ebony curls, his eyes the innocent unbounded blue of the Judean sky. He put an arm around their shoulders and drew them into a circle, which they completed by linking arms; then the three of them spun around, laughing, dancing, and singing. Though the dance was good exercise after their cold immersion, it was his embrace that warmed them all. She remembered Rachamim's face, shining, beatific.

Now it was fallen, no trace of that old joy. Zara said, "But you always encouraged us. Daud used to blame you for throwing me and Raif together."

"You were the nicest thing I could give him."

"I was a substitute?"

"I sure as hell couldn't offer him myself," he snapped.

"Did you never tell him?"

"Stupid!" he called her, then his face softened and he mumbled, "He would have hated me. Despised me."

"No! Of course not!"

"He would have!" She wondered why he sought confirmation of Raif's hypothetical contempt. "You think he'd have been friends with a queer, a homo, a pervert who wanted his ass? Don't you understand anything?"

She was beginning to. The destruction she'd seen in him, the falling apart, the internal bleeding: now he was bleeding from the mouth. She had not, herself, a healing voice, nor a touch like Raif's that set souls soaring. But she hugged Rachamim firmly and said, "If you're looking for shock and disapproval, you've come to the wrong person. All I have is sympathy for anyone who loved Raif."

Rachamim was shaking. After a while he said, "It wasn't true about wanting his ass. Or it's such a small part of the truth it might as well be a lie. I loved him, Zara, just as you did. He had a perfect soul, fearless, open, humorous. How could I risk losing all that by showing how I wanted him? Because I did, Zara. I burned for his flesh under my palms. But now that he's dead, it seems a crime against nature that I never spoke my love, or showed it."

It was a loss that had no remedy, a wound to which no poultice of memory could be applied. She murmured, "It must have been impossible for you when he was killed. You couldn't even mourn properly."

"You can't imagine what went on here. The satisfaction, the gloating. I couldn't work the next day, so I sent word that I had the flu and stayed home. That was a mistake. When you're well, they at least leave you alone; but the minute you're sick and helpless they invade. Of course they knew that Raif was my friend. Neighbors, parents of students, all came rushing over, or else sent their daughters with bowls of chicken soup. Their daughters, my God. I've lived in this village for twenty years and they haven't yet stopped trying to marry me off. Better they should send their sons."

"No one knows?"

"You think I'd still be teaching school here if anyone knew?"

Zara was ashamed. Not that he hadn't told her before. Reserve between friends was a quality that Ronar had taught her to respect. But that she hadn't known. It made her wonder, briefly, what else she'd missed.

When the time came for her final visit, Zara took her father's army revolver and borrowed Rachamim's Vespa.

Uri lived in a small cement house in a new development on the edge of town. She knew the address. He had a wife, Rachel, and no children.

His was the last house in the road. Zara walked the Vespa the last hundred yards, then parked it, facing town. She walked around the outside of the house. Bedroom curtains were open, but the room was empty. The salon curtains were drawn, but she could see through a gap. A house-coated woman sat in an armchair, watching television and talking to someone out of sight.

She rang the bell. When Uri answered she smiled warmly and said, "Uri, how *are* you?" and stepped forward smoothly as she spoke, so that Uri, still uncomprehending, automatically moved back. She pulled the door closed behind her and kept walking. "I've been back for a while and hadn't run into you yet, so I thought I'd drop by"—now she was in the salon; the woman still sat, surprised but calm, in her armchair. Zara took the gun from her bag —"and blow your fucking head off."

"What is this?" said the wife. "Who are you?"

Zara didn't answer. It was necessary to convince Uri she was serious without actually shooting him. A show of force was called for, a commitment to make him think she couldn't back out. She took her finger off the trigger and smashed him hard across the face with the gun, backing off before he could react. Uri buckled, covered his face with his hands. Rachel screamed. "Shut up!" ordered Zara, and she did.

Uri's mouth was bleeding profusely, and his hand, when he lowered it, held a tooth. "You knocked my tooth out," he said incredulously. "Do you know what that's going to cost to fix?"

"Idiot," Zara said contemptuously, "where you're going, one tooth more or less won't matter."

She made him sit beside his wife. Rachel asked between hiccups, "Why are you doing this?"

"Tell her, Uri," she ordered.

"What?" He still seemed dazed. Zara repeated patiently, "Tell her why."

Uri glared at his wife unlovingly. "How the hell should I know? Because she's nuts, that's all."

Zara's voice was low, still patient, and utterly menacing. "Uri, I want you to understand. If you don't do exactly what I say, you're going to die, just as sure as anything. You believe me, don't you, man? Take your hand away from your mouth. I like the sight of your blood. It's what I came back for; it's all I came back for. Now answer your wife's question, and tell the truth."

He told the story of Raif's betrayal, and Zara forced him to admit to his own part. Then, satisfied, Zara said, "And now Raif, my man, is dead. You come from a religious home, Uri. What's the price for a life?" She was standing in front of them, her gun winking lasciviously at Uri.

His eyes widened. "Don't, please, Zara."

"I've got to, Uri. Nothing personal, even. It's necessary. A life for a life. You understand that." She seemed anxious for his understanding.

"Please, Zara, I'm sorry for what I did. I really mean that, and I'll confess—I'll confess that I set him up. If you kill me no one will ever know. Don't you want to clear his name?"

Crafty sonofabitch, she thought, and said: "It was never dirtied, bastard. Don't move!" He'd not been getting to his feet but slipping to his knees. Now he begged, telling her that Rachel was pregnant and needed him.

"Look, Uri," she explained, "I've got to do it. It's justice, man. You believe in justice, don't you?"

"It's vengeance; that's what it is!" cried Rachel. "Wicked vengeance, and for an Arab!"

Zara ignored her. "I'll give you a minute to prepare yourself. Just tell me when you're ready and I'll shoot."

Sweating, crying, and speechless, he gazed at her beseechingly.

"There's just one way," said Zara thoughtfully, "I could possibly let you off."

"What is it?" he cried.

"Instead of killing you, Uri, I'm willing to shoot your wife. Not to kill. Just once, in the knee. It'll cripple her."

Rachel colored, raised her hands to her face and looked over them at her husband, who said, "You wouldn't hurt Rachel. She's innocent. She's got nothing to do with this."

"Innocent victims," Zara smiled, "that's the name of the game."

"You wouldn't shoot her."

170    BARBARA ROGAN

"Choose, Uri. Your life or her legs."

"You can't—"

"Choose!"

"But she's innocent! And I'm sorry!"

"Sorry," she said furiously, "does not bring the dead back to life. Now if I hear one more fucking irrelevant word out of you I'm going to kill you *and* cripple her. You got two seconds, fucker—now CHOOSE!"

"Shoot her," whispered Uri.

"What?" She made him say it again.

" 'Shoot her,' " Zara echoed, and turned to his wife. "Did you hear that, Rachel? Don't you think that's funny? First he begs me not to shoot him because you're pregnant, then he tells me to shoot you instead. Honey, you've got yourself a real man." She started backing out of the room. "Have a happy marriage, you two," and she exited laughing. Just outside she felt a tremor in her legs and leaned back against the door. First there was silence, then she heard Uri's voice saying, nervously, "I knew she wouldn't really shoot you, darling."

# PART III

## IN MOTION

# CHAPTER I

There were silences and silences, and like a blind man she was growing aware of the differences. The desert's silence was that of conserved energy, of life saving its breath. Now, though, in the space between strangers, in the gap between towns, in the pause between adventures, she heard the music of the exile's world: the silence of spent energy. Emptiness.

Other changes. In Ein Gedi she'd scorned the passers-by, desert uninitiates, and, with the rest of the Ein Gedi crew, played King of the Mountain. But she'd launched herself in an opposite world now, the travelers' cosmos where mobility is gold, impermanence glory, and those who were rooted —toadstools.

And she was good. She shone, did Zara, no one could pin her down. Took to the road like a bird to the air and thought for sure she'd found her element: it was called motion. (And the occasional wrench of leaving someone good behind —that she called motion sickness.) There was no liberation like the burden of country cast off. Zara wafted weightlessly over the peasants who'd made the mistake of living in their own countries, and in the upper stratosphere shared nectar and ambrosia with her fellow footloose gods. So it seemed.

It was so much like coming home. They even had names like hers, Candyman, Queenie, the Roadrunner, Gypsy, Freak, who also called himself "The Loner," although he was anything but. They'd met up in Korcula, Istanbul, Amsterdam, and Dubrovnik, and each time he'd had a different woman in tow. First time they met, he briefly tried enlisting her but soon saw it wouldn't work. "For the road I want an adornment, a pretty chick to stop the cars, pass the hat when I play, warm my toes when it's cold, and carry the goods when I'm hustling. Now you, you ain't pretty, you're beautiful, and that's no good for business; you don't want to ball and you're probably running hustles of your own. So who needs you?" They were good friends of the traveling kind. He didn't call her a chick but a woman, which was meant and accepted as the highest compliment, though why he should be the one to hand out degrees she didn't know. He introduced her to people—Freak knew everyone, and his dealing wove a net around the world. He bought carpets in Afghanistan to sell to the yachtsmen in Hydra, dealt Burmese hash in Amsterdam where the stuff was worth a hundred times what he paid for it, sold Bedouin dresses in Paris and Indian silk shawls in Corfu. His face belonged to the caste she called wandering, corrupt Jesuses—high cheekbones, sunken eyes, long blond hair, and a decomposing beauty. He was French, German, Canadian, or Swiss, depending on who was rude enough to ask him; nobody ever saw his passport. He once told Zara a story she chose to believe. When he was twenty-one years old and living in

Berlin, he met a woman, a few years older than himself, and loved her. She said she was English, but her skin was dark, her name was Fleur, and no Englishwoman ever spoke languages the way she did. After they were married, she told him she was a gypsy and, along with the tenderest loving he'd ever known, gave him a warning: she was a wandering soul and would be one till she died. But she would always come back, she promised, and if he was there, good, and if not, that was okay too.

The first time she left him, she returned after four months. She'd been traveling with a band and had a tambourine and an abortion to show for it. The next time she was gone for nearly a year, but then she stayed with him for two. The third time he went after her and didn't find her but developed some traveling ways himself. When he got back to Berlin, he learned she'd come and gone and after that there was little to hold him. Since then they'd been missing each other in place after place all over the globe.

She chose to believe it, even if it wasn't true. Then Freak said, "You're her sister. I recognize you. There's probably some poor guy following your trail right now, never quite catching up."

Zara didn't like it. "You save your romanticism for your own story," she told him severely. "I don't need it." It gave her dreams.

There are rules to being on the road, and a woman hitching alone, through Greece, Yugoslavia, and Turkey, learns fast or far too late. In a pinch she could fight her way out of a rape, or she believed she could, and confidence is the essence. But her roadcraft lay in avoiding trouble. Usually, lone men stopped for her. Zara would amble over, bend down to the open passenger window or door, and say, "Hi, where you going?" And look at the man, at the car.

Was he smirking, looking at her body, was he nervous or too polite? Were there pinups on the dashboard, naked dolls dangling from the mirror? If he said, "Wherever you are," that was easy: she backed off. The crux was in detecting the nuts, who belonged to no particular class or nationality and were betrayed only by the most intangible of clues: an expression about the mouth or in the eyes, tension, an aura of violence or contempt. If the man passed her ten-second scrutiny, she got into the car. There were few who did not harbor fantasies; it was her business to deflect them. Innocence was good but had to be coupled with an aura of invulnerability, a tricky combination. She used a direct look, an innocent smile, an amiable exchange of names. At twenty-three, she could pass for seventeen, and usually did, as empirical trials had convinced her that seventeen was borderline for scruples. It was essential to show no trepidation, no consciousness of potential danger. Once she succeeded in making them feel protective, once they started giving her advice and warnings, she was safe.

When, inevitably, some tried anyway, she stayed friendly but increased the invulnerability component. No one got to lay a hand on her: she'd field the pass before it landed and return a quick command to pull over so that the driver obeyed without knowing quite what she had in mind. Before he knew it, she was out of the car and thanking him for the ride, waving him off as though they'd just dropped her at her own doorstep. Sometimes, crossing Yugoslavia or Greece, her line of travel resembled a diagrammed game of leapfrog, no more than a mile or two with each ride, fifty rides a day. Not the most efficient way of traveling, but surely the most instructive; and though she hitched alone for years, covering tens of thousands of miles, she never met serious danger.

As for companionship, it was as easy to meet people as she let it be. There were the drivers, who usually offered to take her home if that's where they were heading. Sometimes those were scenes worth sampling, but not for more than a day or two before the caged-bird blues got her. Better were the travelers who weren't going home, the ones permanently on the road. She found them within a month of setting out, on the island of Hydra in Greece.

Data accumulated during the month, nodes of survival information that needed to be processed and assimilated, led her to seek a place to settle temporarily. She took a boat from Piraeus and chose Hydra because it was the first stop, and it attracted her. Old women with rooms to rent met the boat, and she followed one to a whitewashed house on a quiet road, just a few minutes walk from the waterfront. Her room was immaculate, and bare, with only a great iron bed, feather mattress, cane chair, and desk. There was a white-hung window with a view of the harbor, and a glass door led to an enclosed garden. Zara paid five dollars for five nights and accepted a cup of scalding, sweet black tea.

The bed was placed to catch the sultry sea breeze, and she lay, tea beside her, listening with closed eyes to the tinkle of donkey bells, the clip-clop of their hooves and carts on the cobblestone streets. There was a smell of jasmine in the air, and the sweetness suffused her body. She was safe, she was warm—she slept.

And awoke hungry, long after dark, to a different set of sounds and smells. She pulled a sweater from her pack, took a key from the old woman, after declining to share her scanty meal, and followed her nose to the shore.

All along the waterfront there were lighted shops and teeming restaurants with tables spilling outdoors onto the pavement. The smell of broiling lamb brought water to her mouth. She'd subsisted too long on store-bought bread, jam, and cheese.

She walked back and forth along the length of the waterfront before choosing her taverna. The one with the white tablecloths and uniformed waiters was eliminated first. Next went one with Greek music blaring from loud-speakers, where all the conversations she overheard were in American. In the restaurant she finally chose, it was hard to tell the waiters from the diners, since they were dressed alike and appeared well acquainted. A great deal of quiet table hopping was going on, with conversations in German, French, English, and Greek.

She was served by an attentive Greek boy of about twenty, wearing blue jeans and a white shirt, whose features were so sweet and yet so masculine that she couldn't help staring. She herself was watched just as attentively by the diners at the table next to hers, a group of four men and a stunning red-haired woman. They spoke English with a variety of accents; and something in their way of treating one another awakened Zara's oblique but intense interest. She had finished her meal and was wondering how much longer she could decently sit there, eavesdropping and watching her waiter, when one of the men from the next table came over and said, "My friends and I have been watching you with admiration. We'd be happy if you'd join us for some retsina."

Zara accepted.

"I am Jean-Luc, that's Brandon, Simon, and the grinning idiot at the end is Roadrunner. This lady is Queen Mary, Queenie for short. Queenie and Simon are married, but the rest of us are free."

"I'm Zara."

"Glad you joined us, Zara." Queenie smiled. "We're

honored," came from Brandon, and the one called Roadrunner said, "I love you, Zara. Come sit beside me."

"Do you fall out of love as quickly as in?" Zara laughed at him, and Queenie applauded: "You've got his number, darlin'."

He leaned on the arm of her chair, and his breath, sweet blend of retsina and ouzo, warmed her face. "Don't mock me. My feeling for you is strong, sure, and eternal."

"Roadrunner!" said Jean-Luc.

"Shut up. From the first moment I saw you, my love, I knew—"

"Roadrunner!"

"Piss off, Jean-Luc."

"Roadrunner, it's your turn to buy the retsina."

"Promise me you'll be here when I return, Zara darling."

Laughter washed through her.

Brandon moved into Roadrunner's seat. He had long blond hair, bound by a beaded headband. "Roadrunner's an impetuous fellow, pay no attention to him. The thing is, we were all intrigued by you. A genuine jade-eyed beauty, dining by herself, an infusion of grace on this otherwise wretched island. . . ."

"A million thanks," said Queenie, with a laugh like water over gravel.

"Forgive my, my lady, your worshipfulness, oh queen of our hearts. Your own beauty is no more spatial than it is temporal. I was referring to the tourist epidemic."

"A singularly poor crop this year," Roadrunner agreed, returning with two bottles of wine, taking Brandon's empty seat with good grace. "Have you betrayed me already, Zara? Hasn't anyone told you that Brandon's gay?"

"*Bisexual*, if you please, Roadrunner, and I feel a definite rise of the hetero."

"Are you a tourist, Zara?" Jean-Luc asked.

Queenie was indignant. "Of course she's not! Would we have asked her over if she was? She's obviously one of us."

"But how could she be, darling?" Simon said. "We've never seen her before, and I've certainly never heard that beautiful name."

"Then perhaps she's a fledgling, but she's certainly one of us. Really, Simon, I don't make those kinds of mistakes."

"By now you've all probably offended her irrevocably," Brandon complained. "Jean-Luc, if she goes away now because of your clumsiness, it's the end of our rather worthless friendship."

"I'm not a tourist," Zara managed to say; they turned to her and waited. She blushed. "I guess that traveler would be more like it."

Queenie's eyes shone.


"And money," Queenie explained, "is the main thing."

They lay on the roof of Queenie and Simon's house, talking and soaking up the last rays of sun while Simon stuffed grape leaves in the kitchen. For Zara the conversation was a sensual delight. It had been years since she had really talked with a woman; the ease of it surprised and delighted her.

"Bumming around is all very well for college kids on holiday, but if you mean to be on the road for a while you need a way of supporting yourself. Nobody likes a moocher, and staying in youth hostels is no fun at all. Now I can't see you panhandling, and that's an overrated gig anyway. What can you do?"

"I don't know. I haven't really considered . . . I have some money saved, that I've been using."

"How much?"

Zara told her.

"Save it. You always need a little nest egg in case you get sick and have to lay up somewhere. Now, be frank, Zara —what are you good at?"

Seeking out underdogs, she thought; but is there a market for that? "I can draw a little."

"Great! Portraits?"

"No, places more."

"What do you use?"

"Pen or watercolor."

"Do you have any of your work with you?"

"A few things. Would you like to see?"

On every street people approached them to greet and embrace Queenie. Zara basked in reflected glory. Without effort, Queenie embodied aristocracy.

She thumbed through Zara's sketches slowly and in the end picked out one of Ein Gedi. "Where is this?"

Zara hesitated. She didn't want her nationality known. Queenie was smart enough, given one constant, to solve equations of three variables. Finally she answered, "Ein Gedi, in Israel," but it was the pause that gave her away.

Queenie said lightly, "Looks beautiful. We've never been to Israel." Zara smiled uncomfortably.

On the way back to her place, Queenie said casually, "We all make such a big fuss about being citizens of the world, free spirits, what have you. Better take it with a grain of salt, love. It's true that we've shed our chauvinism and cut the cords that bound us to our countries. But we've still got our pasts. Your past is your shadow; you can't shed it and it's pointless to try."

"Maybe," Zara said daringly, "you never tried hard enough. Sometimes I feel like I'm getting there."

She'd grown aware, not through introspection but through feeling, of a simplification in her life. There was a lack of reverberation in all that she sensed on the road: experiences pierced her cleanly and deeply, raising neither echo nor reflection, leaving no scars. When she was not immediately sensing, she was still and empty inside. Her mother's voice was gone; so were Raif's, and Rachamim's.

Queenie bought her picture of Ein Gedi and showed it to a friend who ran a gallery in town. He took nearly every picture Zara had on consignment, framed them, and sold them within two weeks. With the money he paid her, Zara rented a small house just behind and above the waterfront town. She painted.

There was competition, less lighthearted than it appeared, for Zara's favors. She chose Jean-Luc, the quietest and most intense of her suitors. It was good, after a morning of work and afternoon of alternating sun and sea, to come home, strip, and mingle bodies on cool sheets. He was a fine, inventive lover, and physical communication obviated the need for verbal.

But suspensions are by nature temporary, and she was careful to move on before dissolution.

# CHAPTER II

Harry's Place was located in the exact center of Korcula. Its exclusivity was ensured by prices beyond the reach of itinerant student tourists and all but the most prosperous locals. But as Korcula was a stop on every seafarer's passage through the Adriatic, so was Harry's the place to start if a man were tracing friends, or enemies.

It was surprising, therefore, when Harry took umbrage at a simple question posed by a stranger. His sharpness in answering drew the attention of half a dozen other men at the bar, attention which the stranger did not seem to relish.

Quite belligerently, Harry had demanded: "What do you want with Zara?"

Unruffled, the stranger examined Harry coolly before answering. "I'm a friend of hers."

"A lot of people think they're friends of hers."

This displeased the stranger, who, however, said quietly, "Who appointed you her guardian?"

"No one; but I'm not the town crier, either," and he walked to the far end of the bar.

A tall, husky blond man beside him at the bar shook his head, and turned to the stranger. "Harry's a bit touchy about the lady."

"Why?"

"Well, it's a long story."

"Have a drink." Two were served, and Harry hovered nearby.

"Zara worked here for a while," said the blond man, "then she left."

"That's not a very long story."

He laughed and held out his hand. "I'm Freak." The stranger shook hands but kept his name to himself. Freak felt in the handshake what he'd guessed at in the man: that his graceful economy of movement disguised considerable strength. He looked European, but his accent was new to Freak.

"Well, if you're really a friend of hers," he said, "Zara showed up here a few months back, out of nowhere and looking for a job. Harry gave her one."

"I wasn't going to at first," said Harry, who, regretting his tantrum, had rejoined them. "I thought she was one of these itinerant hustlers we get coming through here. It was nothing she did or said; I just assumed that a woman with her looks would use them.

"So I asked her straight out if she was looking for a sugar daddy, 'cause I'm not, like I told her, in the business of supplying female crew to yachtsmen. She didn't even answer, just looked at me. So I hired her. . . ."

It had worked well, at first. Zara was good at the work and good for business. Not only did she drew new customers, but the regulars hung around longer and ordered meals, hoping for a chance to talk with her. Harry watched her carefully for the first signs of a hustle, but he watched in vain. Zara was polite to the customers, friendly to a few of the regulars; but she went home alone every night, and if she had a man, he never came into Harry's. So Harry relaxed, enjoyed the boom, and gave her a raise.

When things went wrong, it was like milk souring in a house where a witch resides: hard as hell to trace a causal connection, but without a doubt there is one. Harry hadn't had a fight in his place for five years; suddenly, within two weeks, there were three, and all over nothing. Other things puzzled him, like men making passes at Zara which were intended not to win but to embarrass her. The girl took it well, too well, and therein laid another mystery. Why was this bizarre behavior so unremarkable to her? She never commented about it. Once he drew her aside and said, "I see that guy's giving you a hard time. Want me to have a word with him?" Zara smiled and shook her head. "I can deal with it." "What's it about, Zara? You haven't been encouraging him, have you?" "No," she said, "it's nothing to do with me," and went back to work.

Then there was the incident with Constantin. The wealthy yacht owner had set out to have Zara almost from the moment he laid eyes on her. He began by offering her dinner and ended by inviting her to join his cruise. Zara refused, pleasantly but unequivocally. Constantin postponed his departure once, and then again, to no avail. Exasperated, and unused to losing, he accosted her one night, saying, "Is it the money, Zara? Is Harry paying you so well that you won't leave? Tell me what he's paying you and I'll triple it. Just tell me—I won't even check."

It was the first time Harry had ever seen Zara angry. Her back was to him, and he couldn't hear her voice, but her back muscles tensed like a tiger's, and the quiet words she spoke to Constantin left him openmouthed with fury. Constantin stayed late and got very drunk, served only by Harry. Around closing time, the bartender went out back to dump the garbage and then came around to the front. Zara and Constantin were alone in the bar. She sat at a side table with her back to him, wiping glasses. As Harry entered the bar, he saw Constantin creeping up on her from behind. Unaware of Harry's presence, he paused for a moment just behind the girl, then with a sudden movement slipped one arm around her throat and thrust the other down her blouse. He was very drunk.

Zara's reaction was startlingly competent. She threw herself backward into Constantin. Ignoring the hand on her breast, she used both hands to break the grip on her throat.

Harry heard a voice roar—his own. He had no memory of crossing the room, nor of hitting Constantin; but he must have done both because, moments later, a dazed and bleeding Constantin was draped over the garbage bins behind the building, while Harry slammed and locked the door behind him. When he returned, Zara was calmly putting away the glasses she had wiped. It was, she was, beyond understanding.

The next day she came into his office, closed the door, and leaned against it. "Want me to go, Harry?"

Harry look up, innocently aggressive. "Why? You do something I don't know about?"

"You know why. Scenes like yesterday's. I don't think you need it."

Harry was embarrassed. There was something in all this business that didn't bear thinking about. He said gruffly, "For jerks like Constantin you don't give up a good job.

Now if you're through wasting my time, I've got some accounts to finish."

She smiled faintly; as she opened the door he muttered, "Why the hell did he do it?"

Zara turned back politely. "For that matter," said Harry, more loudly, "why did I?"

"I don't know," replied Zara, and though sympathetic, she clearly thought it his problem.

Constantin's behavior was so unlike him as to be surreal. But what really perplexed Harry was his own behavior. He'd been a fighter once, but since quitting he hadn't laid a hand on any man. And he could not even remember hitting Constantin, though he knew he'd done it. He told this to Zara with some embarrassment. Then, lifting his eyes, he saw her face and added hastily,

"Not that he didn't have it coming."

"Well, there you go." Zara seemed relieved. "You were just dispensing justice. I figure you did him a favor."

"How's that?"

"If you hadn't hit him, I'd have been forced to take out his liver."

Harry laughed shortly. "You would, would you? Get outta here."

The stranger laughed, an odd laugh, soundless but deep, and asked, "Is that when she left?"

"No," Harry answered, pouring himself a drink, "she stayed on for a while. But it didn't work out." He held the whiskey in his mouth for a moment, wiping out a worse taste. "People came down on her, you know what I mean? I swear to God I don't know what for. It was just like one day they loved her, next day they hated her."

"Everyone heard about Constantin and about Harry going berserk," said the blond man. "Zara got the blame."

"They gave her a hard time." Harry was silent for a moment, remembering. "They used to offer her money. It was incredible. And I couldn't interfere because then they just figured it was because she was putting out for me."

"She took it like a trooper," Freak said. "Never saw her flustered, but she never laughed them along, either. As soon as she got some money coming in from her pictures, she gave Harry notice."

"Have another drink," said the recipient of all this information. He seemed little moved by the story, showing none of the indignation they would have expected of a friend. He seemed, indeed, a man not easily moved. Perhaps he'd heard it before. If there was any discernible expression in his cool green eyes, it was one of intense but neutral interest. He said to Harry: "How do you understand it?" and Harry answered as if the question were an extension of his own thought: "I can't. But I guess it's got something to do with the way she looks."

"The way she looks to men, or at them?"

"Both," Freak put in definitely. "It's not her fault she's a beauty, but I wouldn't call it her great good fortune either, belonging to that breed." As the stranger turned to him, he expounded: "Watch a woman sometime, walking down the street. A man comes by and calls out her name, in a glad voice. Does she turn to him with a warm smile and perhaps a slight question in her eyes? Or does she look at him coldly, denying the acquaintance until she's made sure of who has hailed her? The latter is your beauty, gentlemen. It's not pride. She may not even know she's doing it. It's just"—he shrugged—"adaptation to a predatory environ-ment." Freak drank up and concluded: "Beauty's not a matter of degree or opinion, and it sure as hell ain't in the eye of the beholder. It exists, it's real; and the holders of it, the beauties of the world, why, they're a separate breed, gentlemen, a separate breed."

It was there in Korcula, many weeks before the stranger's visit, that Zara first met Freak.

He spotted her one day in town, going softly through the shimmering heat of noon. Unlike most of the women on the island, she wore no sunglasses; a wide-brimmed straw hat shaded her face. She wore white: a shirt of fine linen over bare breasts, loose-belted trousers, and dusty sandals. A gold locket dangled and swung between her breasts as she passed him.

He forgot his appointment with his current lady, Crystal. She drew him to his feet and after her like a yo-yo on a string. When she came to rest at a shady café table, sinking into a wicker seat like a gull landing on water, he took the chair beside her.

She looked him over in a way that made no attempt to avoid his eyes but left him knowing that no contact had been made. Meanwhile, he evaluated her, seeking for vulnerability, a point of entry. What approach would she respond to? It was not at all clear. Beautiful women were hell: give him a pretty girl any day. And there was a complicating gleam of intelligence in her eyes which he dared not ignore.

He broke several rules to ask her: "Would you buy me a coffee?" One of them was never to approach a strange woman with a simple yes-or-no question: too easy for her to say no. But he followed a hunch that the inversion would amuse her.

And sure enough Zara smiled involuntarily, and instead of saying no asked "Why?"

"I left my jacket on the chair of the other café, and I'm too nervous to talk to you without a prop." She smiled again and bought him a coffee, but her first impression was not good. He was too good-looking, all that blond, raucous virility. She sensed a case of self-adoration, a disease she particularly, and for perfectly unexamined reasons, disliked.

"I may be an egotist," Freak said pleasantly, "but not a blind one: witness the fact that I'm here."

It startled her. How had he guessed? "Am I so easy to read?" she asked.

"On the contrary. But I do have a small natural talent for that sort of thing."

"Reading minds?"

He grinned. "Well, I prefer to think of it as reading faces."

She, who had the same talent, shared also the preference. Odder and odder; her sympathy grew. After some conversation, they made plans to meet on the rocks that afternoon to go swimming. He hurried off to get rid of Crystal.

Arriving early, he staked out a secluded section of rock and defended it against all comers. The heat, reflecting off the water and white rock, was extraordinary. Within minutes he gleamed with sweat, which pleased him; he believed it gave his body an attractive sheen. Zara arrived, sat beside him, and began to unbutton her robe. A voice from below, calling her name, distracted her, and she paused, with her hand on the third button, to peer down. Freak stared at the hollow of her throat and the smooth curved flesh of one breast and felt a rising flood of lust. At the same time he laughed to catch himself, with all the nudity around him, peeking down this woman's robe.

Later she lay on her stomach with her face turned away from him. On his elbow, looking at her, he surrendered to an impulse and kissed the hollow in the small of her back. With the honeydew taste of her skin on his lips, he settled back and waited.

She turned slowly and said coldly, "Sweetheart, you've got your signals crossed."

"I know. It just happens to be a beautiful spot, in contrast to the rest of you. Forgive the momentary lapse of iron control. Service is now restored."

"Don't do it again."

"You'll have to beg me," he promised.

This was Freak. Consummate traveler, women collector, and the perfect crew member, as picturesque with a length of rope wrapped around his bulging arm as at the dinner table. A gentleman doperunner, impeccable dresser, international street hustler, self-lover. Freak had a thousand stories, a prodigious memory, and an Irish gift for telling. But friends who tried to put together his life from his stories found that no two pieces of the puzzle quite matched. He was skilled at something Zara had to learn. She liked talking to him.

He constructed his image with as much labor and more patience than Zara had ever put into her painting, he obscured his chronology, and he used people as his media, so openly that they never resented it. His women were careful choices, known for their beauty and connections. In Paris he lived with the fashion model whom all considered France's most beautiful. He was nineteen, ten years younger than she. Her friends declared him a prodigy and adopted him: so that when Freak wrote poetry, it was published, and when he wrote a play, it was produced and attended by everyone who mattered. When he left the model and moved to Barcelona, his coming was heralded, there and everywhere after.

He was as attractive to homosexuals as to women. Though exclusively heterosexual, he did not consider it a bad thing to promote stories of the hopeless passion entertained for him by important men, nor to profit from their unconsummated love. The boat he lived on this season belonged to such a friend, now attending a film festival in France.

Freak was also a naturalist, and beautiful women were the species that he studied. He'd known many deformed beauties, victims of their own reflections. Zara was an interesting anomaly. Her beauty was of an unconventional sort, composed of two challenges: one, a cast of sorrow that graced her face and body in repose, the other, her complete, charming but sometimes eerie lack of self-consciousness. Neither extrovert nor introvert, she was possessed instead of a central silence—or stagnation. Did she know she was beautiful? he asked her many times; the closest thing to a response he could elicit was: "I know that some people have said I am."

"An interesting answer," he replied professorially. "Does that mean that in some people's eyes you are beautiful, or only that for some reason, probably self-serving, they have said you are? Or does it mean, yes, I know I am beautiful, and I see the confirmation in men's eyes?"

She laughed at him, turning discomfort into mockery. "It means nothing more than what I said."

"Don't evade. Do you know that you are beautiful?"

"Don't be stupid. I told you, I know only that some people say I am. To me."

"Then you show," said Freak, "a remarkable inability to draw inferences, to generalize. A strange flaw in a lady who likes politics."

"It's a question," she answered with mock solemnity, "of *need to know*."

Though he wrote and dabbled in theater, Freak's real talent lay in crafting relationships. Seeing that the joy he took in manipulation, the means of his art, was as great as his joy in its product, Zara once said, "You should be in politics."

"But I am."

"And who is your constituency?"

"You are. All our nomadic circle. I consider myself your representative."

"Really? Who elected you?"

"Popular proclamation. I am, you see, fucking good at what I do."

"And how would you define that?"

"Staying loose. Keeping free. We may be the last carriers of freedom left on earth. It ain't in the West, and it ain't in the East. It's on the road."

"How romantic!"

"But not necessarily untrue."

She had learned that people on the road had two reasons for being there—the noble and the personal. Beside defending freedom, Freak was running from the absence of his wife, his gypsy-hearted, gypsy-footed Fleur.

He told her that tale in his cabin. At the end, seeing her sitting as though glued to her chair, while he rolled in seductive agony on the bunk, Freak asked forlornly, "Won't you come over and comfort me?"

She grinned. "You've got Crystal to comfort you." When his efforts to coopt Zara had failed, he had reinstated

Crystal. But he sent her to town during his periodic attempts on Zara, with instructions not to come back till morning.

"I don't want her. I want you."

"I don't know why she puts up with you."

"Don't you? I'm quite a catch, Zara, as I keep trying to explain to you. I've got money and I know how to live well. I've got this boat, and everyone knows I'm an absolute ace in the sack."

"But you treat her so badly."

Freak shrugged impatiently. "It seems she figures the price is worth paying."

"Strange."

"No, it's not. You're the strange one, lady. Everybody else has got a price. You with your independent ways, you're a freak like me."

He saw her stifle a frown at the comparison. With her graceful sprawl, careless sexuality, resolute unconsciousness of their isolation and his strength, she was infuriating. He said, "For a while I comforted myself with the thought that you're a lesbian. Then I heard about Jean-Luc, and Robert, and the others. Tell me something, my little queen of the night, what have those deadbeats got that I haven't?"

She just winked at him.

Angrily he said, "What does it take, Zara, to get close to you? I've tried everything. I've used flattery and honesty, I've revealed myself to you, though you're a blank wall for all the reciprocity I got. If I thought that flowers and jewels would do it, I wouldn't begrudge the price, but I know you don't care about money—your lovers have all been paupers. Is there a certain image of yourself you'd like to see reflected? I'd do it gladly, just tell me what it is. Do you see yourself as saint, repentant sinner, or superwoman? You don't care to be told you're beautiful, but can I offer some other reinforcement? If you want to be a victim I'll rape you, but I don't think that's it. You're no Christian, that's for sure. You do unto others what you won't let them do to you. You're like a poison ivy leaf, with no idea, no fucking idea, of what you do to people who brush up against you."

She tried to placate him: "Look. People lay all kinds of numbers on me. I don't know any way to deal with that except not to."

"That may be," said Freak, "but this ain't just a number I'm laying on you, Zara; it's your number I'm calling."

She said, "Okay, Freak," and stood up. "When I decide to go in for analysis, I'll call you."

He shook his head, anger drained from him, and said, "You're just like my wife. No fucking idea what you do. I bet there's some poor fool like me trailing you from town to town, like I follow Fleur, never quite catching up."

"That's enough," Zara told him dismissively, but no, it was too much. Alone in her bed that night, she had her old dream. Once again she was the Lone Ranger, and her dream prophesied no rest for the weary.

# CHAPTER III

If life on the road is a pleasant kind of death (bonds cut, the traveler floats free above the world, and all the old urgencies just tinkle out nostalgic tunes), and if Zara were a spirit, then she was an earthbound spirit, a ghost, unable to escape the tug of her old passions. Drawn like a mindless iron filing to any political magnet of the proper charge, Zara wisely determined that if she could not escape the political arena she would at least convert from participation to spectatorship. She became a witness and a bearer of witness. What she saw in one country she reported in the next: a carrier of infectious news, she purged herself by telling. Although, or because, she never went beyond a juxtaposed reportage, leaving conclusions to others, her witnessing had considerable value for some people. The combination of ideological simplemindedness with political clear-sightedness gave her a unique mobility through all levels of the left. "Look for the worst possible motive behind any political action, and you approach the truth,"

Ariella used to preach, and her message fell on fertile ground: her star pupil had a nose that could smell out the secret trap behind every perfumed act of magnanimity, the misdirection in every appearance of liberalization. With an eye that was, unwillingly but irremediably, faster than the hand, Zara was the bane of every political magician.

She soon learned that her traveling friends mixed with politics somewhat less successfully than oil with water. When she presented them with the political nuggets that so delighted her, they listened with willing eyes but puzzled faces, as if struggling to recall a language unheard since infancy. "But what's the point?" they would ask if they loved her; if not, they simply nodded with polite disinterest and said things like, "Speaking of Afghanistan, have you heard what those camel rugs are selling for in Paris!"

One night she attended a secret students' meeting, held just outside of Dubrovnik. Ninic, a local friend, translated sporadically. Speaker after speaker talked of freedom of expression, betrayal by leaders, police brutality, political oppression, international solidarity, until she began to recognize the words in Serbo-Croatian. The heat was outrageous: three hundred people were packed into a barn, with the windows blacked out. The speakers drew energy from the crowd and returned it threefold. Then a man rose from the front row and went to the podium, and a whisper of "That's the German; that's Rudi" sped through the room, bringing silence in its wake. There was cold fire in his eyes; his face was very pale and his black hair stood out like a halo. He spoke German, and they seemed to understand. She didn't, but would have followed him anywhere. When he ended, they were on their feet, calling his name and cheering, caution abandoned. Suddenly, and for the first time, the outcome of the evening was in doubt; would they, could they, after this, disperse quietly, go home to their families and their safe studies and their parlor politics?

There came a beating at the door. Instantly the room was still, but the pounding continued, louder in the silence. Rudi slipped from the podium. The doors, bolted from the inside, were giving way. Those outside were using more than their fists, Zara realized, moments before the shiny blade of an ax glinted through the shattered doors. A man screamed. Then the back doors of the barn were thrown open from within, and a mad, scrambling exodus began. Zara heard shouts and commands, a single shot. Then she was out herself and running, across the yard, over a wooden fence, through a field of thigh-high grass. Ninic was gone. She could hear but not see others, also running.

It occurred to her that she should feel fear; she looked for it, but found in its place a most inappropriate joy and a specific confusion. The joy was sensual: it was in the tall, dry stalks scratching her legs as she ran; in the burrs that stuck to her; in her fleetness before the lumbering servants of order and law. And the confusion: a delicate, best-forgotten matter of identity. She seemed to be running in double focus, in overlapping identities. Was she Zara, was she Hope, or was she Ruth, doing what Ruth should have done? There was an extreme rightness in her flight, as if she were completing a circuit whose incompletion had been a low-grade, unacknowledged irritant for as long as she could remember.

She came upon a dirt road just as a carload of students was passing by. They stopped for her. Hesitant at first, because they were all men, she peered at the faces and recognized one: the German, Rudi.

Late that night, unable to sleep, she walked to the harbor to see Freak. For once he was alone. She told him all about it, and when she was through, Freak said, "Pass that joint if you're not going to smoke it."

She took a great toke to counter her astonishment, passed it, and asked, "Is that all you can say?"

"No, I was also going to mention that it's rather obvious you've been running, and if you'd like to use my shower I promise not to come in and rape you."

She was puzzled, a little hurt, but thought she must have explained badly. "See, Freak, there was energy in that place, tremendous energy, hundreds of kids with passion condensing on them, and there was someone capable of harnessing that passion. . . ."

"Zara, knock it off. You should know that local politics bores me to death."

Impossible. She was putting it all wrong. "I didn't mean to say that I was personally involved. Hell, I didn't even understand the language. It was their passion that was so —interesting."

"You mean you'd have reacted the same way to a meeting of starry-eyed fascists?"

She was indignant. "Of course not! The political content did seep through the language barrier."

"Zara," he said, "you're on the verge of a big mistake. Don't get involved in what doesn't concern you. I know what I'm saying. People like us don't mix with politics. It's one of the terms of world citizenship. Look at it this way. The world's our haven. And it's common politeness, if a place gives you refuge, not to meddle in its politics."

He was right, she thought. It was logical. It was what she'd set out to believe. Probably it was only a sexual thing between her and Rudi. She would find that out tomorrow, when they met.

But even after, in a melding of lustful investigation and

investigative lust, she took Rudi as her lover, the thing was
not clear. It was so hard to separate politics from passion.
Lust was not dangerous; admiration was. Rudi tried to
seduce her with his politics; but, though willing to be
bedded, Zara guarded her autonomy. Freak's warning
stayed in her mind, and she would not be lured out of her
stateless haven.

She did agree, after some thought, to act as Rudi's
courier. Why not? She was anyway a wanderer, and it
would do no harm to let her direction be determined
occasionally by purpose rather than chance. There was little
risk involved, and even when she eventually noticed that
people she knew tended to disappear, she never felt
threatened. It evened up her life. Without a map of the
righteous and the unrighteous, where were you? And even
astronauts need a touch of gravity now and then.

In her early enthusiasm she did not give up easily on
snaring Freak. Some weeks after meeting Rudi she strolled
on a bright morning to the harbor, where she found Freak,
bare-chested, scrubbing down the sides of his boat. He
settled her on deck with a chair and a bloody mary, then
went back to work.

"So, Freak," she asked casually, "have you made up your
mind yet about Budapest?"

"Yeah, I'm going next week unless I get a better offer."

"Would you deliver a message?"

"For you?"

"For some friends of mine."

He laid down the scraper and looked at her suspiciously.
"What friends?"

"You don't know them. Isn't it enough that—"

"No, it's not. I'm not sitting twenty years in some cell for the sake of your—"

"Conservation work," she put in hastily. No telling who was on the neighboring boats.

"Hardly that."

She moved her chair closer to him and lowered her voice. "Why not, Freak? It'll be a perfectly innocuous message. And you won't know what it means, so you're safe."

"Safe as houses," he laughed. "It's always reassuring when the walking tornado lady tells you you're safe."

"Why do you say that?" she asked, wounded in her political pride. "I never have trouble."

"That's because you're in the eye of it. Thanks, sweetheart, and I do appreciate your trying to liven up my existence, but find yourself another messenger."

She thought for a while, then said slyly, "It would be fun for you."

He snorted.

"No, really. *I* like it."

"Naturally. You've got all the instincts for it. I bet that when they tap your right knee with one of those little hammers, your left leg jumps."

She laughed. "Thanks. But really you could enjoy it, Freak, if you just play it like a game, like cops and robbers."

"I've graduated from cops and robbers, love. I'm into food and fucking now."

She snorted in disgust and sidled away, looking, he thought, absurdly like a child who's been denied an ice cream. A turn round the desk, and then she was back at his elbow.

"It's not like I'm asking you to do something dangerous like smuggling. You could get caught at that. But is a simple sentence or two too heavy for you to carry? I *know* you want to help."

"That's where you're wrong," he said gently. "I don't. It's part of the life. You see more clearly but you pay by feeling less."

"Are you against us?" she demanded tragically. Knowing that she was manipulating him with her little *moues* of pain, still he found even her mental touch seductive. But the price for pleasing Zara was too high, especially as it was not at all clear that her pleasure would ensure her favors. He answered loftily:

"I don't take stands on temporal things like politics."

"Sorry!" she sputtered. "Forgive me, oh master, for imposing on your peace of mind."

He smiled, but said seriously, "And neither should you. I keep telling you. Nomads aren't supposed to get involved. If you don't see that, you're missing the whole essence of the life. Some people change their states of mind, painfully. We change our states and stay the same."

"Like Peter Pan," she said before she thought. His face registered one shock of pain, high on the seismic scale, and immediately she was sorry, but too late. She'd wanted to believe him; and if she couldn't, she'd wanted to keep her Midas hands off his belief. Freak then cracked a smile and, in a terrible voice, sang gaily: "I'll never grow up, never grow up, not me!"

She was so sorry. It was awkward. Very soon she slipped away.


Her mobility and political aura added to the body of rumor and speculation that was spreading about her. In the small world of the travelers, she had become known as an aloof beauty with an unknown past, whose choice of lovers confounded the rational mind; she was a vagabond, a talented naïve painter, a political Typhoid Mary. Woven of other people's fantasies, the cloak of mystique which she could not shed was growing heavier than the identity she had. Those who envied her the flattery didn't see the danger: if Zara ever saw herself as others did, she was done for. Because they gave her more credit than she deserved. Even Freak in his disappointment credited her with too much. Do-gooder, he'd called her; fanatic, he'd sneered, laughing but seriously annoyed, a teacher whose star pupil had publicly denied him. But there was not a bone of altruism in her. It was not the dissidents' cause that moved her to their side, for of that she had only the simplest conception; rather, it was the ecstasy of the break for freedom, escaping through fields, hiding in forests, doing what her mother hadn't done. And conspiring. Fighting governments who couldn't reach her, because she was not landed and had no people. Freak couldn't see, and she wouldn't confess, that what he called fanaticism was her form of narcissism.

Wouldn't confess: for the truth was woven with the past, and the past, unraveled, would entangle the present.

Zara's political activities widened her wake but shortened her stay in most places. The man on her trail was finding it easier to trace her but impossible to catch up. Not that he minded: the information he was gathering along the way would enable him to control her when, inevitably, he caught her.

By marking her stops and lengths of stay on a map, he identified a loose pattern to her travels. While ranging all over Europe, she favored the warm countries and rarely ventured north after September or before April. She avoided Germany, and though she often stayed long periods in Eastern Europe, particularly Bulgaria and Yugoslavia, she entered Poland only once. The closest he came to catching her was in Warsaw, where he arrived only two days after her departure. It was easy enough to trace her hotel, since she always stayed someplace cheap and central. The desk clerk, a moonfaced man of about fifty, sighed mightily over Zara's picture and bristled when asked for information.

"What do you want with her? What are you to her?"

The stranger's hand went to his wallet pocket, then fell away. "What do you think?" he asked neutrally.

"Her lover," the clerk replied in a depressed voice, "or husband." The stranger assumed as calflike an expression as his hard face could abide, and nodded. The clerk recounted a conversation he'd overheard, in which Zara had accepted a ride to Corfu with a fellow guest.

He had a choice, then, between flying to Corfu and possibly catching up, and finding out what she had done in Poland. Because she had previously taken pains to avoid the country, he decided to stay and investigate. The usual political hangouts—bars, cafés, and clubs—proved fruitless, so he tried the art gallleries, again to no avail. Finally, after several wasted days, he went to the train station and showed her picture there. The second ticket seller he approached recognized her.

"Yeah, I saw her," he said. "Beautiful, beautiful." He raised his eyes to the ceiling.

"Where did she go?"

The man smiled and shrugged; the stranger laid five dollars on the counter and asked again.

"I remember now. I thought, it is strange, you know? Because she did not look Jew."

"What?"

"She bought ticket to Auschwitz. You know Auschwitz? Nazi camp. It's monument now. Many Jews go there."

"Thanks," the stranger said, and turned away.

"Wait. Here, you take back money. Give me picture. Okay?"

She had been two years on the road before she revealed her nationality for the first time. It happened in Rome, where she lived for some weeks with a leftist painter she'd met in Corfu. In a party in some students' loft, she drank a great quantity of arak and, tired of fending off information vampires, retired to an observation post. Beside her, three young Palestinians, a woman and two men, were arguing quietly in Arabic. The woman was defending a friend who had met with Israeli leftists in Paris, while the men claimed that all Jews were Zionists and racists at heart. Listening to the deep-throated Arabic beneath lilting French and Italian conversation, Zara felt as if she were at last turning into the roar of the surf, after hearing only the petty gossip of gulls. One boy with molten-black eyes said angrily: "No Israeli accepts even the existence of Palestinians. They say that all Arabs are the same."

"Your information," Zara heard herself saying politely, in perfect Arabic, "stinks."

While his companions froze, the black-eyed boy turned to her and asked, with dangerous politeness, "And where does yours come from?"

Zara twisted in a trap of her own making. She could not lie in this situation: lies were indecent where the truth was dangerous. Arak cushioned her admission. "I'm Israeli."

"And you speak Arabic so well?" said the woman, but

Zara, hearing her thought, answered, "If I wanted to spy on you, all I'd have to do was to remain silent."

Despite his strictures against dialogue with the enemy, the dark-eyed Arab clearly wanted to continue the conversation, but Zara felt at risk, leaking personal information in a roomful of curious strangers. She said a few quiet words to her Italian friend, and left with the Arabs.

As none of the three had ever been in Palestine, they were refugees from a place they'd never known. Zara felt a fellowship which defied her feeble attempts at analysis. The company of exiles from her own land both exacerbated and assuaged a wound she hadn't known existed.

But she was careful. Where could it not lead? She would give information, but her struggling days were over. When Salim, the dark-eyed militant, asked her to speak to some Palestinian friends, Zara said, "What for? And why should they speak to me? I could be an agent, worming my way into your confidence."

"I've thought of that, naturally," Salim said, "but decided it's unlikely. We're small fish."

"So, perhaps I'm starting at the low end of the food cycle."

"For us it's worth the risk. If your way of thinking represents a segment of Israeli thought, we should know about it. Take it into account."

"But it doesn't," she answered quickly. "Maybe ten people in Israel think like me. Don't change your plans on our account."

Salim stared, his eyes stern and full of judgment. "Do you understand what you're advising me?"

"To do what you must."

Proffered alliance turned instantly to contempt. "We won't bother with you then. You're right; you and your friends don't matter. Especially if, like you, they've all deserted the struggle."

At that they parted, and Zara walked slowly back to her lover's studio. Her confusion and anger polluted the clear Roman sky and veiled the city's midnight brilliance. In one hour Salim had robbed her of Rome, and perhaps more than Rome. Emotion had invaded her perfect sensuality like woodworm attacking a foundation. What had possessed her, to speak to them in their own language? What, except that it was the tongue she shared with Raif, and something deep in her belly yearned for the earthen language of her home. Oh, she could whistle like a Roman bird, charm in French and English, but she missed without cessation or, till now, realization, the dual-tongued language of her land.

Neutrality in one small field, a single DMZ. That's all she wanted and she was willing to pay. Was it too much to ask, that limited apathy?

A fine Roman day in May. Zara sat in a café, eating breakfast, reading a newspaper. Suddenly a man dropped into a chair at her table. As she turned to him, words of dismissal already on her lips, he said in Hebrew: "Good morning, Zara."

Her mouth closed, and she studied him. He was about twenty-eight, with short-cropped hair, wire-rimmed glasses framing dark eyes, a thin, dark face and military moustache. A sabra, she knew immediately, and just the type who could never understand how the European Jews let it happen. "Why didn't they resist? If *I'd* been there . . ." Twice she had seen her father faced with such a statement; each time his face paled, his eyes reddened; his lips had trembled but he made no answer, voice caught between anger and shame. But such memories were rare and unwanted. Zara said in a freezing English tone, "Kindly leave this table."

"Just a minute, Zara," he began. At once she signaled the waiter, who advanced meaningfully. Hastily the man pulled out his wallet and opened it to a Hebrew document. "Mossad," he said, seeming discomposed; "please don't make a fuss." The waiter arrived; Zara looked up and said, "More coffee, please."

Her companion leaned back in his seat. "It's always nice," he smiled, "to find a compatriot abroad." Under her steady gaze his smile wilted; then his face regrouped and his eyes assumed command, grew menacing. "You've been playing in deep waters. We hope you know how to swim."

"Is that," asked Zara with interest, "the royal, marital, or governmental 'we'?"

"You are in a position to help us," said he, and she almost laughed. Whatever made them think they could use her? "We want—we expect your cooperation."

Should she ask what for, or would the question encourage him? Silence seemed preferable, though not to him. "Are you aware," he blustered, "that you could be charged with a serious crime in Israel?"

"What crime?"

"Well, treason," he said, and could not quite hide his discomfort. "Meeting with an enemy, giving information, that sort of thing."

How stupid, she thought, to send this type to her: it could never have worked. Bored with him, Zara said shortly, "Get lost."

"What!"

Her smile was a swift jab to the belly, but her voice drawled. "Don't make a fuss, Mr. Mossadnik. I *can* have you thrown out. So go."

He left. And so did she, that very night for Dubrovnik.

Clearly they had learned of her meeting with the Palestinians and thought to turn it to their advantage. They were buffoons, no doubt, but she had no stomach for their kind. And anyway it was time to move on.

# CHAPTER IV

When Queenie strolled through the *souk*, traffic parted before her like the Red Sea before Moses. Camels genuflected (or would have if there had been any), and hawkers grew melodious. Trailing yards of violet silken shawls, flaming tresses, bandannas, and layers of the lightest, most multicolored skirts, she wended her way through the alleys and secret passages of the marketplace. Little boys fought for the right to carry her purchases; she rewarded them with a plum or a kiss. Fish vendors saved her their best.

When Zara and Queenie walked together through the souk, arm in arm, the traffic did not so much part as melt before them. Zara sensibly wore white in the summer and black in the winter; as it was summer now she was all tan and gold and gleaming white. She wore loose cotton trousers and moved in an uncluttered space, complementing Queenie's brilliant opulence. The Sun and Moon goddesses, they were called locally, in not an unfriendly way.

Zara and Queenie were shopping for ingredients for

Queenie's famous paella. For hours they had wandered by the harbor of Dubrovnik, talking to some fishermen, waiting for the next catch to come in, and choosing the best of everything. When they had finished and sent the fish home with a boy, they walked to the souk for spices and vegetables. Queenie saw her reflection in the eyes of all around them. Admiration was like sunlight to her, pervasive and benign. Zara, when she could not help noticing the fuss being made over them, commented, "They really do treat you like royalty."

"While ignoring you, I suppose?" Queenie laughed. Zara didn't answer; she was looking at some fruit.

"Come into my garden," begged a man who had run up to Queenie. "Have some tea. No charge. It's good to see you again."

"Zara, this is Demarjian, a friend of mine. Let's have tea." In his garden café, he served mint tea, chatted for a while with Queenie, his back bent in an almost ninety-degree angle of deference, and then withdrew. Zara closed her eyes. The sounds of the souk grew stronger all around her, stronger and older. Unseen, it was very like Jerusalem, another walled city, much defended. Zara was moved to tell Queenie about her encounter with Salim, though it meant confessing finally her nationality. Why did she? It was something to do with the quality of their friendship, which, having gotten under her skin, harried her with a sense of past deprivation: for it was a childhood kind of friendship, all dressing up and playing out fantasies and telling secrets; and it was her first.

As she began the story of the meeting in Rome, she felt to her horror tears gathering in her eyes. Had they been acid, the sensation could not have pained her more. If she had not cried then or *then* (rather than remembering, her mind stabbed blindly backward, indicating times, not events), tears now were unforgivable. She stopped speaking, breathed deeply, concentrated on the mingled smell of mint and roses, drew mental lists of ingredients for the paella —but nothing helped. The tears rolled down her face. In her mind she heard the refrain of an old Israeli children's song: "It's not me who's crying, Mama, it's my tears." Finally, she looked fearfully at Queenie, prepared for embarrassment, and saw instead the tenderness of one woman recognizing another's passion. It was the look she had shared with Ariella the first time they met. Neither spoke, and in a few minutes the tears ended. Queenie, a delicate friend, asked no questions, but by her silence demanded that Zara go on. She did, telling of Salim and their talks, and ending: "I told him there were no other Israelis who think like me. I told him to go on hating."

The sun was low and the market was closing. But they sat on.

"It's not true," Zara confessed. "I don't know why I lied," and Queenie said irrelevantly:

"Why don't you go home?"

Home. There were nights, she couldn't deny and wouldn't admit, when she woke in the dark, in a strange room, choking with anxiety. Where was Rachamim now? What had happened to Ein Gedi? Where was Raif buried —she didn't even know. Had Ruth repented? Foolish thought. Were they looking for her, or was she forgotten, erased?

And yet return was not an option. For even if she wanted to, she had no right to forgive wrongs done to others; and such wrongs! No right to forgive, no heart to struggle, and only a hollow semblance of pride which she used to answer Queenie. "I don't have one. Or need one."

"Maybe you do."

"You and Simon don't."

"No, but like the silly songs say, we've got each other. Anyway, for you I don't think a man is enough."

"I want independence."

"What for?" Queenie's voice was suddenly sharp. "So that when they lay you in your grave, they can write on the tombstone: 'Here lies Zara, dependent on no one'?"

She started and her mind darted backward. "Trust no one," she heard her mother say. "Depend on no one. Build nothing on the benevolence of others. Only your family cares." She'd believed it.

Through the still, sea-laden air came a sudden cypress-laden wind from the east, with a tang of desperate loneliness, bad decisions, lost moments. It came from afar, Zara swore it to herself: this was not her loneliness, not her desperation. For it is axiomatic that the homeless know no exile, feel no pain: what else is the point of renunciation? She was an orphan, a war orphan. She bowed her head, for the wind had condensed, leaving tears on her face, and blindly reached for Queenie's hand.

The sun was down, and there was a sudden chill in the air. Somewhere from among the folds of her costume, Queenie produced another shawl and offered it to Zara.

Simon, Queenie, and Zara were eating supper one midnight on Zara's little balcony. They had come from a concert.

Queenie sipped red wine and said, "I loved the Mozart."

"You would," said Simon.

"I liked the Bartok," said Zara, and Simon replied:

"Naturally."

"Did you hear, Zara, that Freak's back in town?"

"No, really?"

"Yes, Claude saw him yesterday. He's traveling with a girl he picked up in India."

"Is she Indian?"

"No, but she's about twelve years old."

"Queenie," said Simon warningly.

"Well, she's quite young, Claude said. American, I think."

"Did Claude tell him we're in town?"

"Yes. I'm sure he'll be by soon."

Just then there was a knock on the door. Freak came in, bearing wine and roses, with Claude and a beautiful, straight-haired Alice-in-Wonderland type of girl who looked no more than fifteen. He hugged Simon, kissed Queenie's hand, squeezed Zara and kissed her on the lips. Zara put more skewers on the fire. When she was introduced to Freak's friend, the girl said, "Oh, wow!" Zara looked at her in some surprise. "I've heard of you," the girl explained. "I know some people who know you."

She said no more, but for the rest of the evening made Zara uncomfortable by gazing at her with awestruck eyes. Freak was amused.

He helped her clear the dishes. This was such un-Freaklike behavior that she was prepared when he said with elaborate nonchalance, "By the way, Zara."

"Yes, Freak?"

"Did that guy ever find you?"

"What guy?" She was rinsing dishes; he moved so that he could see her face, at least in profile.

"The one who was looking for you in Korcula last June, and in Corfu after that."

She turned to him, smiling, expecting a prank. "I don't know what you're talking about."

As if speaking to a defective child, Freak said slowly, "Last June in Korcula a man came to town on business. You were his business. Brandon ran into the same guy in Corfu, a few months later. I was hoping you'd run into him because I sort of wondered who he was."

Zara stared, doubted, believed. Her face grew instantly hard, as if covered with brittle transparent glue. "What did he look like?" she demanded.

Freak lit a cigarette and offered one to Zara. His eyes never left her face. "Brown hair, my height. About forty. I wouldn't want to mess with him. Looked European but had a non-European accent that I didn't recognize. Do you know who it is?"

She shook her head and looked worried.

"Well, I suppose that's a relief."

"Why a relief?"

"I thought he might be your husband."

"I'm not married!"

"After I met him, it occurred to me that I'd never asked if you were or not."

"I'd have told you."

"Would you?"

"Why should you imagine he was my husband?" she wondered, thinking that it must be someone else from the Mossad. There was no one from Israel who would look for her, except her mother.

"Some old lover?" suggested Freak, and Zara laughed.

"You imagine a lover, and I'm immediately sure it's an enemy."

"That *is* interesting," Freak said. He wasn't laughing.

Then he said gallantly but absently, as though his thoughts were on something else: "But you couldn't have enemies."

"I've told you that you're a romantic." Zara spoke severely, in the tone in which Ronar used to tell her, "You're a dilettante." "Of course I have enemies." She was slightly resentful. Who was he to deprive her of her enemies, and where would she be without them?

"I don't," Freak confessed suddenly. "Where do you get them?"

"You have to settle someplace for a while. They grow."

"The rolling stone gathers no enemies, you mean. Am I missing an experience?"

"Well, yes, you might like to add it to your collection some day; but then you have such a large collection."

He smiled and she felt a trap closing in. "What will you do when your current crop runs out? Settle down and raise some more?"

"I don't need them."

"Of course you do. I think enemies are like oysters —absolutely delicious; once you get the taste for them, it's addictive."

"What nonsense, Freak! You're getting senile."

"In what kind of soil do enemies grow best?"

Though the conversation annoyed her, she couldn't help answering: "Native."

The next morning, when Zara awoke, she went directly to her one full-length mirror and studied her reflection.

A dream had remained with her upon awaking, and it carried not only its own content but also the knowledge that it was recurrent. In the dream, she stood naked in front of a mirror, as she did now, examining herself. Her reflection seemed strangely smooth and virginal; she was used to lying reflections, but this one showed that something was definitely missing. Suddenly she realized that her body lacked a navel.

It was a ridiculous idea, but still she looked at herself when she awoke. Upon reflection, the dream was less bizarre than it had seemed, for what was the navel but a scar? And other scars healed.

# PART IV
## AT REST

# CHAPTER 1

Tony waited at her gate. He was a little early; she would be a little late. His eyes were on her window, curtained, but he could imagine her behind the opaque cloth, drifting through the room. The wind blew lightly down the mountain, carrying the smell of melting snow, running water. He turned into it, let it dry the sweat that always covered him on these waits outside her gate. One day she wouldn't come. But not this time. He felt himself harden, and pressed against the cold iron gate.

Soon she would come, unlock the gate, take his hand or press his cheek. In her house, there would be a fire, a table laid for two, the fragrance of pine and cooking food. His mouth would water, but he'd lose his appetite. While she worked in the kitchen, he would pass the time staring at the fire, tantalizing himself with an image of her naked body on the hearth rug. How could his rough hands touch that silken body? But they had, and would.

They would eat and sip wine, sitting close enough to

touch, not touching. His nervousness dissipated by her eye-spoken acceptance and liking, they would talk. At first he had been embarrassed. He was only a bank teller, seventh son of a Chicano father and Indian mother. He'd never even been out of New Mexico. But she seemed, she was, interested in him.

She told very little about herself; he thought this was not elusiveness but forgetfulness. She had been, it seemed to him, all over the world. In places that were and would remain nothing but sounds to him, she had lived, paid rent, taken buses, and shopped in markets. She had absorbed and forgotten these towns and countries. And men.

She was the farthest from a virgin he had ever known, though his experience was not wide. He could imagine her having princes and revolutionaries for lovers, artists, philosophers, and fools. He thought he was her first bank teller. But they had passed through her, and whatever they had left of themselves was not in her memory. Though they had seeded her, the seeds hadn't taken, or were dormant. After dinner they would lie together before the fire. It didn't matter then that he too would recede from her. Only the soft flesh of her belly pressed to his, and the feel of being inside her, mattered.

It was astonishing, he thought, waiting by her gate, a thing that would never be believed. Ever since she'd come to town, he'd heard about the men who tried to have her. Maybe Santa Fe was a hick town to her, but they were important men in his world. Not one had made it through those gates.

She'd opened an account at his bank; that was how he'd met her. When she came, she favored his station.

Miguel noticed, and teased him. "It's that angel face of

yours, lover boy. Maybe she goes for children. Why don't you give it a try?"

Mr. Massey, the assistant manager, overheard and laughed unpleasantly. He'd invited her several times to skip the lines and bring her business directly to him, and though she'd smiled and thanked him politely, she'd also ignored the offer. "Give the kid a break, Miguel," he said. "He wouldn't have a clue how to score with one like that."

He hadn't. It seemed just to happen.

One night she came in alone to the Forge where he was playing for the first time. She took a table near the bar, and he knew she was a regular by the way the bartender looked after her, serving her drinks at the table and keeping the macho flyboys off.

He played an unplanned version of "The Girl from Ipanema" for her, trying to put something into his sound about the way she looked, the way she moved, the way she moved him: things he would never dare say.

Zara knew what he was doing by the shyness that kept him from glancing in her direction. When the set was over, she sent the bartender over with an invitation to join her.

First she said, "I guessed you had a secret life. I like your music."

Everybody was looking at them. Why did she have to do this? Crucifixion through kindness. Couldn't think of anything to say; finally he muttered, "Do you play?"

"No. I listen."

What a stupid question. Now she would think that he felt superior, because he played while she just listened. But she was smiling, easy as an old friend, and didn't seem to mind if he sat dumb all night. "I like it," he said simply.

"I can tell."

"Can't make a living from it yet, though."

"Not yet, anyway. Not here."

"There's these guys in Albuquerque who want me to come and play with them regular. They're good. But they don't make a living either, and the bank won't let me transfer till I've been there two years."

"Albuquerque's not so far away."

"About sixty-five miles. I get down there about once a week to play with them. I'm going Friday." This time there was no response from her, but the slightest drawing back. Hesitantly, he asked:

"Would you like to come? I have a car, I could take you. . . ."

She hesitated, obviously looking for words to refuse. He thought, what a fool! How dare I ask her, like she's some kind of high school pickup. He blushed and hid his trembling hands under the table. Zara said gently, "I'd like to hear you play. But I don't feel like leaving Santa Fe just now."

"Sure, of course, you've got better things to do than—" He stopped because she was laughing.

"I don't actually. It's just that if I leave right now, I might keep on going, and then who would look after my dog and feed my horse? Why don't you come play for me in my home?"

Just like that. He felt like Joshua watching the battlements fall from just a riff on his horn.

He was a modest boy, but perceptive. In time he gained a feeling of what she needed in him. A link, someone she could open up herself to without risk.

Not a lover. They made love but he was not that to her.

He was more—a lifeline.

Solitude had become, not a place she sought, but a state

she lived in. Chained to herself like a prisoner to his cell wall, she had felt the rising waters of solitude reach her breast till she could not feel; reach her mouth till she could not speak. The waters reached her eyes, and sight gave way to vision. One day, riding her horse through the arroyos, she heard familiar laughter and looked to her left: Raif was riding beside her on his uncle's white Arabian stallion. There were tears in his eyes, which could have come from the wind. His lips moved, but his words were blown away. Though she strained to keep her eyes on him, when she blinked he was gone. Overwhelming desolation was tempered in her heart with a sense of tender, invisible regard. In a dream she heard the words the wind had stolen: "Come home," he had said. "Come home." She ignored the summons. Even ghosts could err.

She had hoped that her long odyssey had ended, that Santa Fe could become her home. The terrain, with its rocky land, scrub-covered mountains, and sandy arroyos, reminded her of Tivon, but Santa Fe was colder than any place she'd known, and favored with more snow and rain each year than the Galilee saw in a decade. Its people were strangers to her, she to them. One third Chicano, one third Indian, and one third Anglo, the town was vitalized by racial tension, in which she felt at home and from which, belonging to none of the ethnic groups, she believed herself exempt. It was the best place she had found since coming to the United States.

What finally drove her from Europe was the *Doppelganger* effect. She wouldn't otherwise have chosen to leave. Of course there were times, stranded on a mountain road or carred-in with a bore who was going her way, when she thought of quitting. But the life had its own impetus: she had a vested interest, a nonconvertible investment to

protect. Wandering, she'd acquired skills that were useless
in any other life. She could pack all her belongings in under
fifteen minutes, carry her life's savings in the heel of her
boot, leave lovers behind with barely a backward look or
the loss of an hour's sleep. Nor was she altogether immune
from the generic contempt of the express train rider for the
sleeping or toiling earthbound laborers she passed. Why
leave a life she excelled at?

But there were so many Zara legends floating about that it
wearied her, time after time, to deny them. Her reputation
as a not-so-secret courier of the left gave credit where none
was due, caused danger where none was necessary. But
worse yet was her absurd miscasting as a *femme fatale*. It
meant that there was always some fool about, eager for
self-immolation, and others, perfect strangers, determined
to bring her down.

Seeing herself through the prejudiced eyes of strangers
was like living in a houseful of distorting mirrors. She could
not follow Queenie and Freak about forever, and in the long
spaces between friends she encountered a new form of
silence, a hum of disconnection. The stories people told her
about herself were Circean seductions designed to entrap.
She was not what they said she was; but when she felt her
certainty wavering, she chose flight over surrender. By
coming to America she hoped also to lose her persistent but
ever-lagging shadow, the man whose identity she could not
penetrate but whose nationality she suspected.

If she could not lose a shadow in New York, well then,
there was need for basic reassessment. She came with little
money, her only possessions those she carried on her back.
On the day of her arrival, Zara settled into a dingy
residential hotel in the Village. Street people, well wrapped
up and lounging on stoops, commented on her arrival. That

was all right, reminding her of places she'd lived in in Italy. But the price of even her cheap hotel room and the cost of a hamburger and Coke dinner were shocking. A French art dealer had given her a list of galleries and dealers whom he knew and a letter of introduction. She began visiting the places on her list.

It wasn't having her work turned down that hurt. She was untrained, it was to be expected; success would have been surprising. But within a few days she understood that New York had a way of refusal by devaluation that made her feel foolish for trying. *"Who* are *you?"* they said, or thought, or hinted with raised eyebrow and that strange, skeptical smile peculiar to New Yorkers. "What makes you worth my time?" Her letter was treated with contempt. "So you sold some stuff to tourists in Europe. Where have you exhibited here?" She'd explain that she had arrived only days earlier, but the explanation offended. "Look, dear," she was told, "it doesn't work like that. You don't hop off the boat, open your portfolio, and expect all New York to flock around. This is the Big A, not Poughkeepsie. Come back when you've got some U.S. exhibitions under your belt, and we'll have a look." Those who did look didn't comment; her work, their silence implied, was irrelevant. Weeks went by; her money was low, it was bloody cold, and she was living on jam sandwiches.

She knew no one, but Rudi had given her the name and phone number of a political associate living in New York. She contacted him.

Their first meeting was short. . . .

Michael was gray-suited, short-haired, horn-rimmed and weak-chinned, a Jew in his mid-twenties; he shook Zara's hand and said, "Any friend of Rudi's . . . He's a good man, doing some important work." She was astonished by his patronizing tone; Rudi was a force, not a "good man," and he'd single-handedly vitalized thousands of political slugs.

Michael had a pouting mouth, which gave him a pompous but childish look. "Of course we don't always agree with his methods; we feel that the ration of talk to action is in his case a bit too high, but there's no doubt his vision is pure. I've checked with my colleagues, and they've agreed to let you come to a study group tonight. I'll pick you up at eight. You'll find it interesting," he said, reminding her of the Lufthansa pilot who announced: "Good morning and welcome to Lufthansa flight 264. We are flying at an altitude of 25,000 feet. You must enjoy the flight. Thank you."

He picked her up in a van whose back windows had been blacked out. Zara sat alone in the dark interior while Michael drove in circles for forty minutes. When they arrived at last, he opened the back door of the van and hustled her into a building, muttering gleeful apologies for the necessary security precautions.

There were eight people in the apartment, five men and three women. One of the men approached them as they entered. Unlike Michael, this man wore jeans and a workshirt. Despite his filthy nails and attire, Zara's nose twitched at the powerful smell of privilege he emitted. Michael introduced them, showing great respect to the second man. He was called Moses, and though she did not react to the name, he explained sharply, "I'm not a Jew. I was given the name to symbolize my function in the revolution, which is to lead my people to freedom." His eyes dared her to show doubt, but she knew better; her face registered polite interest as she wondered who had given him the name.

"You say you're a friend of Rudi's." Exaggerated skepticism, intended to insult.

"Yes."

"Been long in the States?"

"Two months."

"You speak English well." Too well.

"Thank you."

"How was he doing, last time you saw him?"

"Quite well."

"When was that?"

"Six months ago."

"Are you a member of his organization?"

"No. Sometimes I worked as a courier between his and others."

"Why weren't you a member?"

She felt some annoyance with this young man who seemed younger with each question. His obvious distrust amused but also appalled her. Where were his eyes? His nose? If he could not sense the difference between enemy and friend, what would this inept interrogation avail him? But no trace of her thoughts appeared on her face as she answered patiently, "I had sympathy but no conviction, and I've never been prepared to accept party discipline."

"Where are you from?"

She exploded: "That is *really* none of your business!"

"Moses" nodded and abruptly switched roles, from interrogator to stern initiator. "We have no time for sympathizers. You're either with us or against us, and you'll be called upon to make that decision very soon." He turned away, but before he did he ran his eyes deliberately up and down her body. Zara's nostrils flared as she smelt his thought: he had her down as a revolutionary concubine and meant to teach her discipline.

Michael tapped her arm, said apologetically, "We have to be careful, you know. They're constantly trying to infiltrate and entrap us."

"They?"

"The feds."

"Really? What would they do if they caught you?"

"Shit, what do you think?" He shook his head at her naïveté and boasted: "Knock us off, most likely."

"They're that scared of you?"

"Shit, yes. We've got a lot of popular support. There's thousands of people out there waiting for us to lead the way. There's the whole fucking black population of New York City, plus all the spics who haven't sold out, and a few righteous honkies." Everyone in the room was white.

"How do you organize so many people? Do you send members out to meetings in their homes?"

"Are you crazy? We'd be busted in a week, dead in two. We talk to nobody but our own, and maintain our cover. As far as anyone outside knows, we're just your average war-loving, nigger-hating, money-grubbing citizens."

"I suppose," she said respectfully, "you've spent a lot of time in prison?"

Behind his horn-rims his eyes glittered scornfully. "Not us," he said. "Getting busted blows your cover. Besides, our kind don't get busted; they get shot."

"No shit. Lost many friends that way?"

He glared and said, "Take a seat. We're beginning."

The subject for the evening was "Exxon and the CIA: Who's pulling whose strings?" Zara had sat in on many working groups in Europe that were like shareholders' meetings: long, meticulous, rather boring reports of who owned how much of what, where the hidden financial interests and points of power lay. Now she heard unsupported supposition presented as inside information, and the most commonly quoted source was the magazine *Rolling Stone*.

Later, thinking of Ariella, who braved the not inconsiderable wrath of the authorities every time she took a case, Zara asked about their methods to learn about their courage. They answered that their task was to maintain a 100 percent politically pure leadership cadre, in preparation for the day when the boiling cauldron of capitalist contradiction would spew them forth, and they could be revealed in their glory as revolutionary leaders. Zara didn't understand the answer but they were all glaring at her, so she tried another tack. "Do you have the support of the unions?"

Unions! they cried. Hard hats and desk clerks! Bribed watchdogs of the capitalistic manger! What would we do with the support of the unions! As they muttered in contempt, she risked a third question. "I would like to get my bearings. Your ideology—is it basically Trotskyist, Leninist, Maoist . . . ?"

"This is our ideology!" Moses roared, and with a sudden sweep of his arm he swept the table clear, sending beer bottles and ashtrays crashing to the floor. "Right on!" cheered the women revolutionaries, scurrying to clean up. "And this is our support." From a pocket he drew forth a revolver, slammed it onto the table. A Luger, Zara noticed, and none too clean; there was lint sticking to the barrel. "Very impressive," she murmured, smiling. As far as she could see, these graduates of the Mickey Mouse Club believed that all you needed for a revolution was guns. She awaited the climax of the show when the doors would be flung open and Mouseketeers, armed to the teeth and juggling grenades, would make their entrance for the grand finale. But the voices droned on and on, with nothing to break the monotony of unrelieved, unrelated fantasy.

# CHAPTER II

New York battered down her pride but captured her interest.
She had no other reason to stay. The extreme isolation in
which she found herself illuminated the city around her, but
most of the light cast was upon the recent past. Certain
forms of relating, which had been too pervasive to be
discerned during her travels in Europe, were defined and
realized by their absence in New York. For example: there
were times when she was hungry enough to trade on her
appearance for a free meal. Getting the usual brush-off from
an agent or gallery owner, she would say sadly, "That's too
bad. I'm having a hard time with this town." Then stop and
simply look at him.

In Europe, any man, and most women, would respond to
such an opening by inviting her to talk over a meal. In New
York they gazed back blankly, focusing several inches in
front of her face. It could never have occurred to them that
she was hungry; if it had, they would have done nothing but
hasten her departure. Their terror of imposition came, she

supposed, from overcrowding or overcompetition. Sex, to the extent that it existed, was so devalued that she couldn't get a doughnut for a smile. But not only sex: she herself was presumed valueless until proven otherwise. A terrible existence, but each day of it gave more value to what she'd left behind.

She learned: one can live without harm among strangers in Europe. But a stranger in New York has no way to balance the daily erasures of nonencounter. If ten million people said she didn't exist, who was she to claim that she did?

For Zara, nonexistence was a sexy lover: she flirted with it, never really feeling endangered. On New Year's Eve, she spent $2.50 to see *Casablanca* near Times Square. When she came out, close to midnight, masses of people were streaming toward the Square. She pulled down her hat, turned up the collar of her trenchcoat, and set out against the stream. Every unseeing face that passed took a piece of her with it. When she arrived at the hotel, she was cold, empty, and somewhat frightened, which comes from playing Humphrey Bogart with nobody there to watch. Where, it seemed necessary to ask, was all this leading?

The desk clerk handed her a folded note with her key. She held it in her fist until she reached her room and locked the door behind her. In the next room someone was moaning. She read, "Zanav called," and laughed, recalling her mother admonishing her, "Don't mix languages, Hope. It's vulgar." "Zanav" in Hebrew meant "tail." How dared he announce himself: what contempt it showed! Did he think he'd cornered her, salted the bird's tail?

Her enemy, who was tied to her inexplicably and, seemingly, inextricably, despised her. Bent on sabotage, he would saw off any branch she tried to settle on. And he knew what was in her mind.

And if that was so, then he'd reckoned on the weakness that threatened her now. He'd divined how the city would affect her and how she would respond to his offensive. Her enemy had her at a disadvantage: he was making her laugh. That her single source of self-recognition should be her shadow was an absurdity that threatened to burst into fondness.

Unfit to fight, she was too well trained to attack from weakness. She would find herself a position, eventually; in the meantime Zanav's appearance could safely be taken as a sign that she was not meant to stop here. Okay. She hadn't much liked it anyway. She could live better on the road than in the city, though she had grown tired of wandering.

For months afterward she traveled around America, stopping occasionally when a town attracted her or she needed money. Waitressing jobs were always available, and, in the places she chose, a new face and strange name were novelties enough to give her an edge. She stayed long enough to place her somewhere between having stayed and having lived, and then moved on. Nothing ever tempted her to settle, certainly not the men she sometimes took up with, until she came to Santa Fe.

Santa Fe was meant to be the end. From the moment she saw it, she loved the town. Cold it was, but full of light, a taut bright town with enough hostility to buoy her, but not enough to bury her. It was like quenching a thirst noticed only when quenched: she realized her physical yearning for the land she'd grown up in only when she found one like it.

A few days after her arrival, she was dining in a Mexican restaurant, finishing a cheap, delicious plate of enchiladas.

Near her sat three men, clad in boots, chaps, and wearing cowboy hats they hadn't bothered to remove, talking about work. The two younger men apparently worked for the National Park; their companion, an older man, with gentle blue eyes in a weather-beaten face, ran a riding stable. He said, "My stableboy's gone off to Taos, left me in the lurch. You guys know anyone who's looking for a job?"

Zara finished her coffee, laid down three dollars, and went over. "I happened to hear you're looking for a worker. I need a job, and I'm good with horses."

His two companions exchanged glances and grins, but the older man returned her look with one that was courteous, sad, and doubtful. He said, "Well, I don't know . . ."

"I'm stronger than I look."

The two boys whooped; he frowned at them and said, "I bet you are, miss. It's just, I was just thinking you could do better for yourself. Job pays okay but it's hard, dirty work."

"Give me a try. What can you lose?"

With a nod at the empty seat, he invited her to sit. They talked some more, and it was settled. Zara started the following day.

Ray Santos ran a small riding stable at the end of Canyon Road, bordering on the national forest. He taught children and took groups of vacationers riding through the Reserve. The upper crust of Santa Fe society, the Chicano gentry and Anglo artists, stayed away, for in Santa Fe, riding was not the status sport it was back east, but rather was associated with the working class: to say that a man was stuck to the saddle meant that he lacked either ambition or good sense.

Ray Santos had lost his wife not long ago, a slow and suffering passage that had left him tired. It wouldn't have surprised him to learn that Zara too was mourning someone,

for she had an air of bereftness about her. But she hadn't
much to say. Once he asked her where she was from and
saw confusion enter her eyes, and then laughter, as though
she mocked her inability to give a simple answer to a simple
question. And when he saw in her that perplexity of simple
things, he felt they had met in the wilderness.

He gave her work and a more than decent wage, and
helped her find a place to live. That was not difficult, with
all the houses left empty by summer visitors. She soon
found a house she liked. Set back from upper Canyon Road,
the adobe cabin had fireplaces in the bedroom and living
room, and a cast-iron stove in the kitchen. A tall adobe wall
hid the house from the road. She bought a new padlock for
the wrought-iron gate, and took possession.

From six in the morning until two she worked in the
stable, cleaning, feeding, watering, and occasionally exer-
cising the horses. Afternoons, she was free to walk or ride
through the mountains and arroyos surrounding the town.
Quite soon she began to paint.

In Santa Fe, certain mountains were sacred to the
Indians. Only months after she started going obsessively to
paint on Monte Sol and Monte Luna did she learn that these
two hills were held the most sacred of all. She had never
believed that land could have religion: dirt was dirt, she had
argued in Israel, and dirt neither worshiped nor believed.
But her attraction to these two hills among all others led her
to conclude that, though rock and dirt were agnostic, they
could conserve the change of men's beliefs. Even the
sacrilegious act of painting on holy ground seemed to
release energy into her work.

The Sangre de Cristo range was grander by far than the
Golan Heights, but the arroyos of Santa Fe were the wadis
of her youth. She began to paint her memories, taking risks.

She set up her easel on Monte Sol, overlooking the barren
hills of Judea. In every one of these pictures was a hiding
place, each landscape overlaid a secret narrative, an unseen
drama. In one pastoral picture, invisible, illicit lovers
embraced behind a rock; their veiled passion informed the
visible landscape. Another mountain scene showed the
black mouth of a cave. Though unseen, a presence could be
felt by the emanations of rank fear and bitterness that
seeped from the cave and infected the foliage: a fugitive
sheltered there. In pictures of the Golan foothills, whole
armies were encamped on the far side of the hills, betrayed
by nothing more than the fluttering tip of a pennant which
could pass for a kite.

The pictures sold, but there was little joy in that.
Something was happening. She hurt all the time she wasn't
working. Her suffering gave her the kind of gentleness that
comes upon the dying; inwardly, she wrestled with angels,
demanded audiences with God. That delusive gentleness
did her harm among the townspeople, when those who were
drawn toward the gentleness ended up feeling that they'd
poked a sleeping tiger. Her self-absorption made her
insensitive; she turned down invitations that should have
been accepted and rejected advances with more brusqueness
than was wise. In a short time, without noticing how or
even that it happened, Zara was left alone. Her pain never
took the form of depression but was characterized by a kind
of puzzlement. Something was needed and she didn't know
what. Tony was an outlet and an inlet, her one small
window on the world.

The trouble, she believed, was that once you stop
running, things catch up. All those years on the road, she
had lived so firmly rooted in the present that she'd thought
she'd lost her past. Never thought of Tivon, never thought

of Rachamim, Raif, Ariella, or her parents. Ein Gedi was a
constant longing never identified. Her mind had been a
stream; now, at rest and stagnant, it was a pool, and every
pebble that touched its surface sent out expanding rings.

For example: Americans, she'd noticed, liked to say,
"Come the revolution . . ." In all the times she'd heard it,
the phrase had passed over her like a rolling wave. But in
Santa Fe it broke: "Come the revolution," she heard a young
man say, and it sent her through mockery and out the other
side, back to her Israeli war.

Memory was more vivid than experience had been; and
strangely, in her memory, she experienced her mother's
emotions more strongly than her own. Zara came home one
day to find Ruth dressed in black, sitting on the floor and
weeping: and so knew the anguish of her father's death
before it happened. Ruth called it appeasement, the staving
off of catastrophe. None of Zara's pleas for sense could
penetrate Ruth's unshakable expectation of the worst. She
would hear nothing but the English broadcasts from Leba-
non and Syria, which recounted tales of Arab victory, the
destruction of the Jewish army, the crushing of the Zionist
state. When the Syrian radio announced the capture of
Jerusalem by Jordanian forces, Ruth believed it—even after
Zara made her phone friends in the city.

Later that night, the third night of the war, Zara awoke to
the smell of burning plastic. In the kitchen she found her
mother pouring ashes down the sink.

"What did you burn, Mother?"

Ruth looked at her distractedly. "Our identity cards." She
slipped an envelope into Zara's hand. "Take these and keep
them with you. If anyone asks, we're American tourists
here on a short visit." When she saw what was in the

envelope—her American passport and birth certificate—
tears came to Zara's eyes. "If only," Ruth cried, "our name
weren't so damned Jewish!"

A week later, the war had been won and Henry had called
home, safe and sound. The moment she accepted the fact of
Israel's victory, Ruth so totally forgot her panic that she
spent the whole of one morning searching the house for her
identity card.

Zara kept in touch, as well as she could, with her
European friends. Indeed, with cheap airline flights as good
as bridges, she saw more of them than she'd dared hoped;
but her visitors were like oases at which she could never
drink enough.

Having Freak to stay was like having a highway running
through her house: there was a constant draft and the smell
of the road about him, and a dazzling foreignness to his
speech. He appeared without warning one day, a few
months after Zara had settled in Santa Fe, explaining that he
was on his way to Mexico, but accepting with alacrity her
invitation to stay for a while. He bore a gift, a hand-carved
Buddha about ten inches high, glazed to a hard black finish.
Zara took it dubiously. It was not beautiful, merely an
expensive souvenir, not to her nor, she'd have thought, his
taste. He grinned at her but remained obstinately silent,
waiting for something other than thanks. Lifting the carved
figure, she found it surprisingly light. The black glaze
disguised the figure's substance. She brought it to her face,
sniffed, looked wonderingly at Freak and sniffed again. He
laughed. "I don't believe it," she said.

"Try it then." He tossed over his pocketknife. "You can
hollow out the inside. No one will ever know."

Laying the statue on its side she cut into the base.

Beneath the thin layer of glaze, the Buddha was made of a deep brown, earthen material. She tasted it. Excellent hash.

"Did you bring this through customs? You didn't dare!"

"Three of them," boasted Freak; "it was reasonably safe. If they're at all suspicious they look for false bottoms, but this is obviously carved of a single piece. I declared them and paid sixty dollars in customs."

"No one asked what they were made of?"

"No. And I must admit I was prepared to lie if they did. They had no reason to suspect. In fact the customs man quite liked them, and offered to buy one at the price I declared. I turned him down. Where will you put it? I'm afraid it's a bit tacky for your decor. This house, my dear, is perfectly Zara."

Whatever that meant, she thought, but agreed that it was a good house. A bedroom, studio, and kitchen, unadorned whitewashed walls, polished pine floors, bare except for several scattered Navajo rugs. Austerity was tempered with a few vivid splashes of luxury: Zara's bed was a simple foam mattress on a raised wooden platform, but her linens were blue satin.

She was embarrassed by how few people she knew. On his first weekend, she arranged an outing on horseback for Freak. Saturday morning at daybreak, she and Freak, Tony and Ray loaded Zara's horse and three others into a van and drove up to Aspen Basin. It was a clear cold day and the oat-fed horses were sharp and eager. Zara's silver shepherd bitch, Moonshine, ran by her side as they cantered into the aspen forest. The ground was slightly frosted, springy, perfect for running. Amid the swaying of the aspens the trail was like an imperfectly concealed revelation, a fluid way. Zara hit her stride and felt invincible, trusting that the path would open up before her. She felt graceful, but appeared slightly mad. Glancing back, she saw Ray close behind her. Though he rode effortlessly, guiding his horse with just the shift of his weight, he didn't seem to be enjoying the ride.

Suddenly, the wind veered and the aspens parted, to reveal a bull standing on the path, with head lowered, only fifty feet away. Zara drew up her horse and shouted back a warning to Ray. When he placed his horse neatly in front of hers, blocking the bull, Zara felt a rush of admiration and a momentary, weak-kneed pleasure in being protected. Tony and Freak caught up and they flanked her, both looking embarrassed to be doing it but unable not to.

"Git on," Ray snarled—she could only imagine he'd learned the tone from TV, because Ray was a Chicago boy. "Gah!" he yelled and slapped a coiled rope against his thigh. With a contemptuous look, the bull slowly turned aside and wandered off through the forest. Ray grinned back at Zara and in a deep Western drawl said, "Nothing to be scared of, ma'am," to which she replied: "It wasn't me, suh, it was m'horse."

Later they stopped to eat and rest the horses. Tony and Zara ambled off, and when they came to a sheltered copse, stopped, embraced, and kissed. Zara was struck dumb and dizzy with pure sensual grace; Tony was thinking that it was the first time they'd touched in the light of day. Later he was happy as a bride when Zara took his arm in plain sight of the others.

Freak approved heartily of Tony. The first time they met, he followed Zara into the kitchen to whisper, "He's fantastic! What eyes! Where did you find him? Is he intelligent or just pretty?" "He talks," she answered dryly. Freak felt no jealousy: Tony was too obviously a part of the scene, like Moonshine and the horse, and indeed he felt a vague pity for all three. Not that Zara meant any harm. Her affair with Tony was still a secret from the town, guarded by each for the other's sake. Freak hoped they would keep it so: for if not, when Zara left, retribution would fall on Tony.

Freak stayed ten days, a short reprieve for Zara; when he left she felt desperately alone. There was no remedy in town, for by now solitude was expected of her, no changing of roles in midstream allowed.

Tony was good for her, he was good, but goodness was no answer to her needs. She couldn't imagine what was.

There came the day in Santa Fe when she saw Raif riding beside her. He was dead, of course. She knew that. But why, having taken the trouble to return from the dead, was he calling her home? It was, after all, he who had sent her away.

Her pursuer, too, was drawing near; she felt his thoughts bent on her, increasing in strength as her confusion drew him on. She was sure now that she knew him, but recognition was blocked.

It came to her one day, a short time after her vision, that her pursuer was Raif. In a fantasy sprung full-blown from her mind, Raif had not died in prison: he had escaped, but before he could contact her, she had fled the country. This was torment, and she reasoned thus with her delusion: if it were Raif, he would have left his name someplace, so that she would have stopped running and gone to him. And even if, by some miracle, it were Raif, then so what? *They* were dead, even if he wasn't. The innocent he had loved had been blown to pieces in Tivon and Ein Gedi; the innocent she'd loved could never have survived prison unchanged. Her friend Tony was an innocent, and that was the true source of their inequality. If Raif came back as he once was, she would swallow him whole. Better stay dead, she advised him.

The thought that it could be Raif she was fleeing was at once so unlikely, and so painful, that she recognized it as a form of self-torment; but it was bigger than she and her precious rationality. Once the fantasy had her in its grip, she could not run again, though she disbelieved it. And, as though they had lain waiting for this moment of weakness, demons attacked her; if only she could really call them demons and exorcise them. Fantasies: sitting at home reading, she sensed a moment in which the quiet slipped from peaceful into threatening. She heard the lock on her gate clink open and heavy, slow, booted feet approaching her door. A leather-muffled fist pounded on wood—her book slipped to the floor. *"Open!"* I will not hide, she thought, as her legs carried her to the door; and, this cannot be happening. An Aryan stood there. His blond hair glinted in the moonlight, his teeth gleamed above his black uniform. "Let me in," said the wolf, and she, hypnotized little pig, did it. "Are you the Jewess Ruth Ronen?"

Then Zara awoke and thought, wait a minute. If this is my fantasy, why is it my mother's name? She didn't know, how could she know, that Zara's fantasy was Ruth's memory.

Of course it was not Raif. No boyish lover, much less a dead one, would follow Zara through Europe and across America. This man is devoted, a hunter of skill, patience, and intense focus. However this started, it's no game now. He's a tracker but he's never had a quarry like this one, a chimera who changes shape as she moves. The woman he will catch is not the girl he set out to pursue. He has observed her changing reflection as he trails behind, and perhaps he could have caught up before. Why didn't he? Was it merely her reflection that he sought? Collector of her portrait on the retinas of other men: it was a strange kind of intimacy he'd achieved. Perhaps he had just been waiting, with a hunter's patience, for just the right reflection, one with that hint of vulnerability drawing him in.

It was hard to remember what exactly had started him off after her. What drew him on was passion, neither love nor hate but a passion of the intellect, an overwhelming interest.

He'd learned this: that while she knew a great deal about the road, she knew nothing of herself in the world. Perhaps it was her total lack of self-consciousness that strengthened the image she cast. Passionate desire, irrational hatred were not, to her, rare spices but daily fare; she made peace with it by believing that the world was charged that way. That's why she could never cover her tracks. He'd long since learned to recognize her spore, the shell-shocked expression of men who'd known her briefly.

He knew her so much better now. If it had been him, trying to lose himself, with a face and presence like hers he'd never have chosen a town like Santa Fe. But she was not made for American cities, and with that self-indulgent innocence he'd traced across the country, she'd think herself well-hidden here. Of course she stuck out like a mermaid in Kansas—but she was always stupid in that respect.

If he'd understood her in the beginning, he could have skipped the laborious tracking and instead sought out her natural habitat: found the place where she would be most foreign and staked it out. Santa Fe in the off-ski season was an even mixture of old Chicano blood, hick Anglos, and oppressed Indians. She couldn't be more out of place, or in her element.

From a distance he'd sensed her fatigue, and it drew him in. In Santa Fe they knew her face and pointed out her house, a small adobe place with an adobe wall higher than the roof and a locked iron gate. They called her the sad-eyed lady and said, "That's one who doesn't care what gifts you lay by her gate," and some said, "Good luck, buddy," but didn't mean it. There was a difference to her presence here that quickened his heart. Here she had stayed for months, rented a house, bought a dog and a horse. She had quit running. This, then, would be the site of their confrontation.

It was hard to remember what he'd wanted when he started. But he knew what he wanted now.

# CHAPTER III

Solitude and immobility: the combination wore her down. The visions and fantasies told her she was too much alone. So she began to spend more evenings in bars and cafés, not to meet people—she was emitting a force field now that kept them off—but to watch and overhear them.

One night, sitting in a corner in the Canyon bar, she saw news from Israel. Another in a series of terrorist attacks, but this one was different. Even as the newscaster spoke, Zara imagined the scene. Four Palestinian guerrillas infiltrated Israel from Jordan, rowing silently over the Dead Sea on a moonless night. The first settlement they came to was the Ein Gedi kibbutz. Choosing a house at random, they broke in. The kibbutznik, Haim Almog, whispered to his wife, grabbed a pistol from the night table, and rushed into the front room. Before he could fire, he was shot in the shoulder and disarmed. Nili, his wife, had meanwhile grabbed the baby from her crib and ran into her son's room. Because he had measles, he was sleeping at home instead of with the other five-year-olds in the children's house. Snatching him from his bed, she dragged him, her hand over his mouth, back into her bedroom. In the front room she could hear excited voices speaking Arabic, but not her husband's voice. Pushing the boy down, she pointed to the floor under her bed. But the moment she turned him loose the child skirted past her, crying "Daddy!," and ran into the front room. She swayed, swallowed a scream, and turned to the baby, who was beginning to whimper. Underneath the bed, Nili lay on the infant to stifle her cries. In the front room her husband suddenly spoke, pleading in broken English for the life of his sons. And now the boy screamed, not in fear but in pain, and she knew then that they were all going to die. To save the baby, Nili throttled her till at last she lay quiet; then she listened for the sounds of rescue. A neighbor, roused by the shooting, rushed over the lawn; they killed him as he opened the door. Next door his wife screamed out his name. All the kibbutz was stirring now, and men called out to one another, searching for the point of danger. The Palestinians conferred and decided to run for Jordan with their hostages. As they opened the door, the voices of the kibbutz men grew shrill and pointed, like hounds in first sight of the fox. First, Nili heard her husband shout, "Don't shoot! Hold fire!" Then she heard shots, and then silence.

Father and son, said the newscaster, were killed by the terrorists, who in turn were killed, two in battle and two after surrendering, by the kibbutzniks. These, when they entered the house, were first surprised not to find two more bodies, then joyous and thankful when the woman emerged, still cradling her infant, from her hiding place. It took some time before anyone noticed that the baby, too, was dead. Smothered.

It took Zara time also. At first she felt nothing but a slight chill, which surprised her because the bar was well heated. She wanted to leave, but realized as she tried to that the chill was in her, and it was growing, had already deepened to turn her body to brittle ice, sharpen her senses to icicle points, and numb her feelings. Freezing was not unpleasant but she was afraid that one harsh movement or undisciplined thought would shatter her. So she sat very still, staring at the table, and thought not at all, but only listened. At the bar a drunken woman in a red satin dress and cowboy boots sobbed loudly and asked, "How will she live? That poor woman. How will she ever live?" A man told her to shut up: "Amy, you're getting disgustingly soppy." The words hissed and changed in Zara's ears: disgustingly soppy, soddenly soppy, a mess, a bloody mess.

Then the noise of the barroom faded out, and Zara succumbed to a succession of vivid, unrelated memories.

During her stay in Ein Gedi, Zara often visited the Bedouin Mustapha. Once he told her a story which she knew could not be true. If you tear a cactus from the ground, he said, nine times out of ten the plant will die. But every so often a strange thing happens—a plant whose roots have been destroyed goes on living. These rare specimens sustain their rootless existence by turning carnivorous.

When Ruth got out of Auschwitz she weighed under seventy pounds and had eight different diseases, but she was far from death. She was cared for, impersonally but efficiently, in an English hospital. Within a year of her release, everything visibly wrong with her had been cured.

Back when Zara was still Hope, attending grade school in New York, she was thought by her second-grade teacher to be seriously disturbed. The teacher wrote to Ruth: "Hope is an intelligent child but something is blocking the expression of her intelligence." Henry and Ruth fought bitterly over that note, and Hope, a skilled eavesdropper, heard every word.

"How can you call this anti-Semitism?" Henry cried. "The teacher's name is Epstein—she's a Jew!"

"There are Jews, and there are Jews," Ruth replied. "She hates Hope because Hope is the daughter of Nazi victims."

Henry groaned. "Talk sense, woman. How could she blame Hope for being the child of innocent victims?"

How indeed? Not even Ruth understood the mechanism of punishment.

When she found she could move again, Zara went home. No one spoke to her or noticed if she looked strange. Her house was cold, so she built a fire, moving carefully. Wrapped in a blanket, she sat before the fire and grieved.

She imagined she was the mother. Impossible to live, bearing the crushing memory. Death would be kinder, but it was far from her to seek that kindness. She could not live, but would not die.

She imagined she was the child, the mother-smothered child. Anger, terror, agony, and sorrow clung to the spirit, binding it to earth. But the spirit itself wept to see the mother's pain. Could anyone blame the mother, used as her enemies' agent to murder her own child? Was any heart cold enough to withhold pity, bestow blame?

Zara's tears went on and on, she had no power over her grief, nor could she understand it.

The fire was out long before she fell asleep on the floor, wrapped in her blanket before the hearth. Even then she cried in her sleep and awoke with tears on her face and a strange, full-blown, newly conscious desire to see her mother again.

He stood outside her gate, note in hand, wondering at the height of the adobe walls. They made sense, but which sense did she have in mind? She offset her foreignness by keeping a low profile, but some women upset men just by existing and she was one of them. So perhaps they were protection.

Or they could be meant to guard her from him. That she knew she was being pursued he had no doubt: it showed in the increasing canniness of her moves from town to town. But that she knew by whom—he doubted. Hoped not. The chase she'd led him had been long and serious, never coy.

But finally he decided that the walls were not a defense at all, but a statement: fair warning to all would-be scalers and invaders.

He stood there, knowing she was inside, not ten meters away. If he chose, he could vault over the wall and see her now. But he was too skilled in the ways of wild creatures and made his plans craftily. First give gentle warning, then let curiosity draw the creature in. Speak softly and carry a hidden net.

He slid the note into her mailbox and raised the little flag. In a language not much used in Sante Fe, he'd written: "Through a strange chance I find myself in your town." For the first time, for the sense of conclusion was strong in him, he signed his real name, and as an afterthought added the name of his hotel.

Then he waited, and on the second day found her note in his hotel box. "Truly a strange coincidence," she'd written, and he heard her laughter; "I must meditate on it." Then, against all the urgings of his hunter's instinct, he could wait no longer and went out to find her. And she was there, standing as if waiting across the road in the town square.

She had in some wondrous way taken the very attitude in which he always recalled her: still as a tree on a windless day, staring down at the earth, her body carving out of air a composition of longing and fear, concentration and isolation. He crossed over to her.

"Zara."

She lifted up her eyes and he saw laughter in their depths. "Aren't you," she asked, "the man who kicked me out of bed?"

And she took Ronar home.

Later he took her home.

But not easily, not without a struggle. For Ronar was a cold and determined lover, not a man to contemplate failure; all his patience was predicated on eventual success. And Zara, though summoned home incessantly on so many fronts and by so many voices that she could hardly hear the present for the clamor of the past, was determined to resist. Thus the courtship was no romantic pas de deux, but an apache dance, brutal and uninhibited. When it suited him, he even used words of love—she would not stoop so low. Words of love, in his calloused voice, recalled his gentle hands on her bruise, the hard press of his body joined to hers in flesh and in thought: moments of revelation, disregarded and forgotten. They made love. Lying beside him in the after-weakness, she could not ignore the memories laid out with their entrails open for reading. But she said: "You never loved me."

"You were a child, a wounded animal." It was no answer.

"That didn't keep you from sleeping with me."

He had a wolfish grin and he laughed without a sound.

"I'm no saint. Wasn't it good?" She had to admit it, but insisted: "I was always aware of your indifference."

"You were never aware of anyone's feeling except, sometimes, your own. If you felt indifference, it was yours."

Using the truth was low, dirty fighting, not what she expected from Ronar. But why not? Hadn't he castigated her for failing to use her sex in the fight against Yoav?

"When," she asked dauntingly, "did you allegedly start to love me?"

He replied, mocking her: "When you threw the coffee into Beni's face. But then it was retroactive."

Impossible memories were being dredged up. She left him in bed, and went into the kitchen to make coffee. But he followed, and stood behind her, pressing her to him. She refused to look at him, finally said angrily, "I have enemies in Israel! How can you expect me to go back?"

"You flatter yourself," he said. "You can't really ___m them as enemies, living here."

She pulled away. "I don't want to claim them as enemies. That's the whole point. I've had it. Read the papers—look at what's going on there now. I don't want to fight anymore, and I won't live there and watch in silence."

"You'll have to choose one or the other."

"I don't *have* to go back."

He turned her around roughly and glared into her eyes. Her robe had fallen open but he closed it. He was pale, and his fingers dug into her skin. "I have decided to marry you. I will be more than your lover, I will be your ally. I've a better idea of the enemy now and won't be used again. We would make an effective team. But Zara—I tell you this because I know you're blind to it. Even if through some terrible error you refuse me, you must go back. You need a home. You're a type whose passion is for places, nothing else. You need Israel. You're a child of the Middle East, wherever you were born, and you're fit for no other land. Listen to me! In this we're alike: it's neither race nor religion to which we belong, it's climate, place, and people."

She cursed and wept but could not deny it. He was only saying what all the voices said. Zara sublet the house, sold the horse, kept the dog, parted from Tony, and went home.